LAUGH FUNNY

# Shoot, Dad!

## Michael Coleman

Scholastic Children's Books,
Commonwealth House, 1–19 New Oxford Street,
London WC1A 1NU, UK
a division of Scholastic Ltd
London ~ New York ~ Toronto ~ Sydney ~ Auckland

First published by Scholastic Ltd, 1994
This edition published by Scholastic Ltd, 1996

Copyright © Michael Coleman, 1994

ISBN: 0 590 13360 8

Typeset by DP Photosetting, Aylesbury, Bucks.
Printed by Cox & Wyman Ltd, Reading, Berks.

# CONTENTS

*To Stephen,*
*my favourite footballer*

# CHAPTER 1

## Rock-Bottom Rumney

"Shoot, Dad!"

As he watched the bulky, red-shirted striker charge towards the opposition's penalty area, Simon "Swot" Watson yelled as loudly as he could.

"Shoot!!"

Swot knew what should happen now. It was obvious. He'd seen it on video hundreds of times.

Wembley, 1966. England against West Germany, in the World Cup Final. The last minute of extra time. Bobby Moore strides out of defence and passes to Geoff Hurst. Hurst starts running. On and on he goes, holding off a defender as he ploughs his way into Germany's penalty area.

WHAM!

Hurst blasts the ball left-footed into the roof of Germany's net. England are the World Cup winners!

OK, so today was a bit different. Rumney Town against Barfield United was no World Cup Final. The tiny Rumney Town ground certainly wasn't Wembley. And Rumney weren't 3-2 up either; the score was 0-0.

Nor was Rumney's gangly left-midfielder, Norman Adlam, any elegant Bobby Moore. But, for all that, his through pass *had* put George Watson in the clear and so, as far as Swot was concerned, his dad only had to do what Geoff Hurst had done – bang the ball into the net.

"Shoot, Dad!!" screamed Swot again.

As if following instructions, George Watson pulled back his left foot and shot.

He hit it well. Nobody could deny that. Even Geoff Hurst himself couldn't have hit it harder.

But he could certainly have hit it straighter. "Oh, no!"

Swot groaned as he saw the ball sail over the Barfield crossbar, over the rickety wooden fence that surrounded the Rumney ground, and land high up in the branches of a tree.

"Close," said a voice at Swot's side.

Swot looked at Kev Murrant with surprise. Kev didn't usually aim compliments in his dad's direction.

"It was, wasn't it," agreed Swot.

"Yeah," said Kev. "Close to going into orbit." He pointed away across the pitch to the Rumney bench. "Looks like that's what Fred Olney thinks as well. He certainly doesn't look too pleased with your dad, does he?"

Swot had to admit that Kev was right. The Rumney manager had thrown his cap on the ground and was jumping up and down on it.

"What good's that?" said Swot angrily. "A decent manager doesn't show his feelings, even if he is under pressure."

"Which he is, of course," said Kev. "Lose

3

this one and Rumney are down. Kaput. Relegated."

"Not true," said Swot. "Mathematically, we can still stay up."

But it would need a miracle, he knew. Two more defeats and Rumney were down for sure. They were desperate for points. Even a draw against Barfield would help. Just as long as they didn't lose.

"Not much fun, being a manager," said Kev as Fred Olney picked up his cap and slumped back on to the bench with his head in his hands. "I mean, you can dish out the best instructions in the world, but at the end of the day you've got to leave it all in your players' hands."

"Huh!" muttered Swot.

"Or do I mean all in your players' feet?" said Kev.

"Hands, feet," said Swot miserably, "what difference does it make when they're Fred Olney's instructions. A half-witted chimpanzee could do better. I mean, look at that!"

While the disgruntled-looking Rumney

groundsman had trudged off to find a ladder long enough to reach the top of a tree, the game had restarted with a replacement ball.

From their goal-kick, Barfield had swept into the attack. A quick exchange of passes in the centre of the pitch had left the lanky Norman Adlam miles out of position and given the Barfield right back plenty of room to go on an overlap down the wing.

The full back hadn't got far, though. In a desperate attempt to recover the situation, Adlam had charged after him and gone for a sliding tackle with the aim of putting the ball into touch. Unfortunately he'd only half-succeeded; he'd missed the ball, but put the Barfield right back into touch.

"Look at that!" repeated Swot. "There was no need for it. All Norman Adlam had to do was jockey him out towards the corner flag. Easy. A good manager would drum that into his players."

Kev nodded. "Still, at least they're getting a wall sorted out," he said as four Rumney defenders lined up to block the free kick.

"I don't like it," said Swot.

"It looks all right to me."

"It isn't," said Swot. "They only need two in the wall for a free kick out on the touchline. Any more than that and they're going to be short of cover in the middle."

"You sure?"

"Positive. Watch."

They watched. And, as Kev suspected, Swot was right.

As the ball was swung over, Rumney *did* find themselves short of cover in the middle of their defence. Panic set in.

Rob "Corky" Corcoran, the Rumney goalkeeper, started to come off his line. As the ball curled away from him he went back again. Finally, spotting the queue of unmarked Barfield forwards waiting for a free header at his far post, he changed his mind again and definitely decided to go for the ball.

"Keeper's!!!" he screamed.

His call came too late. George Watson, also seeing the lack of cover in the Rumney penalty area, had raced back to help.

"Oh, no!" groaned Swot as the two players collided in mid-air.

"Oh, blimey!" groaned Kev as the ball ran loose to the Barfield striker who only had to tap it over the Rumney line for the easiest goal he'd ever scored.

"That was Fred Olney's fault," said Swot.

"Fred Olney?" said Kev. "It looked more like your dad's fault to me. Him and Corky the Cat."

"He only came back to help," said Swot. "That wall should never have been wrong. That was basic. You sort out things like that in training. No," he said grimly, "we're one-nil down because of bad management."

Kev didn't argue. Trying to convince Swot that his dad had done something wrong was a battle he knew he could never win. Sooner or later Swot would blind him with science. He always did. Probably, thought Kev, because he'd read every football book that had ever been written. That was why they called him "Swot", after all.

"Maybe you should get over there and tell Fred Olney how to do it," said Kev.

"Fred Olney doesn't need telling how to do it. He needs the push. Rumney needs a new manager."

"Too late, now. Maybe next season."

"By which time we'll have been relegated," snorted Swot. "Thanks to Fred Olney."

He looked at his watch as Rumney restarted the game.

Four minutes to go.

If only they could equalize. At least that would be one point in the bag.

From the kick-off, George Watson laid the ball back to Norman Adlam and hared off upfield as he called for the return. A Barfield defender saw the move coming. He easily intercepted the through ball, then laid it gently back to his goalkeeper to boot upfield.

Three minutes to go.

Barfield were moving forward again. The Rumney defence retreated. The Barfield striker took the ball out wide and wasted a bit more time near the corner flag until Rumney's captain, Terry Potts, was forced to give away a throw-in.

Two minutes.

The Barfield striker took the throw himself, sailing it high and long into the Rumney penalty area. This time, Corky Corcoran made a better job of things, leaping up to pluck the ball out of the air. Then he immediately undid all his good work by slamming the ball wildly upfield without looking to see where his forwards were positioned, so that a Barfield defender had no trouble in simply heading the ball into touch.

One minute.

It's got to be now or never, thought Swot.

Norman Adlam threw the ball to Terry Potts. The Rumney skipper, off the field a burly police sergeant, moved forward to throw his considerable weight into a last-ditch attack.

He took the ball on, past one tackle, then another. A third defender came to meet him but Potts shrugged him off with the ease you'd expect of a man who'd once put a would-be bicycle thief under one arm, the bicycle under the other, and carted them both back to the police station for questioning.

With another couple of giant strides he reached the edge of the Barfield area. He looked up.

The Barfield centre backs had retreated, either because they didn't want to tackle him, or because they weren't sure they'd live to tell the tale if they did.

Terry Potts seized his chance and shot.

Whoosh! The shot was unstoppable. Even Peter Shilton at his best wouldn't have sniffed it. Into the net it flew.

"Goal!!" yelled Swot.

"Yaahhoo!!" whooped Kev.

Then, from the Rumney bench, came what sounded like a cry of agony.

"I don't believe it!" screamed Fred Olney.

The man's a nutcase, thought Swot. His team's just scored and there he is, looking as though he's about to have a fit. Suddenly he discovered why.

"Offside," groaned Kev. "The ref's disallowed it."

"No!" exclaimed Swot. But he soon saw that Kev was right. The linesman on the far side of the pitch had his orange flag held high in the air. And the referee wasn't pointing to the centre spot as he should have been. Instead he was pointing to a spot much nearer the Barfield goal.

"And guess who it was?" said Kev.

Swot didn't have to.

The referee was pointing straight at the bulky, red-shirted culprit with a number 9 on his back. George Watson had strayed offside at the crucial moment. Terry Potts' goal hadn't counted.

The whistle blew twice in quick succession.

Once for Barfield to take the free kick.

Then a second time to signal the end of the match.

Rumney had lost.

Again.


Swot and Kev were standing dejectedly out-side the faded wooden clubhouse which served as the Rumney Football Club's changing rooms.

It wasn't hard to tell which team was in which changing room.

From behind the door marked "Away Team" came a happy burble of talk and the odd outbreak of laughter. The noises coming from behind the door marked "Home Team" were quite different. At first they heard nothing. Then came the sound of an angry

voice, a voice they'd heard a lot of that afternoon.

"Fred Olney's giving 'em some stick," said Kev.

"I'd like to give Fred Olney some stick," muttered Swot.

The manager's voice raged on for a couple of minutes. Suddenly it stopped. Moments later Swot and Kev knew why.

Fred Olney, with his even-flatter-than-usual flat cap jammed firmly on his head, stormed out of the Rumney changing room. He hurried past them, to the small car park alongside the pitch where his car was sitting in a spot marked by an old oil drum with the word "Manager" painted on it.

"Fred is not happy," observed Kev as Fred Olney started his car with more noise than Nigel Mansell revving up for a Grand Prix. "Not happy at all."

"Nobody would be with him as manager," said Swot, as Fred Olney's car screeched away from its spot with a smell of burning rubber.

Another screech, this time as Olney

brought his car to a halt, wound down the window and stuck his head out. "Shoot, Dad!" he yelled at Swot. "Shoot, Dad! If I had my way I'd shoot the ruddy lot of 'em!"

And then he was gone.

# CHAPTER 2

## Farewell to Fred

George Watson emerged from the changing room ten minutes after Fred Olney's furious exit.

"Bad luck, Dad," said Swot, as he and Kev followed him across to the old delivery van which had passed as the Watson family's transport for as many of his fourteen years as he could remember. He jumped into the passenger seat.

Kev was pretty sure that luck hadn't had much to do with it, but he wanted a lift home – even if it was in a van with "George Watson, Greengrocer" painted on the side in bold red letters.

So he echoed, "Yeah, bad luck, Mr Watson," and jumped into the back of the van with its heavy smell of fruit and veg.

Not that George Watson looked as though he was going to argue. He clearly had other things on his mind as he slammed the van's rear door shut and got into the driving seat.

"What a ref!" he said immediately. "Crikey, I've sold spuds with better eyes than him! I tell you, lads, if I was offside then I'm a Dutchman."

Kev almost said that George Van Watson sounded pretty good, but as they weren't moving yet he kept quiet.

Swot's thinking took a different direction – such as how Rumney could do with a few real Dutchmen in their side. Ruud Gullit and Marco Van Basten, for example, who'd helped Holland become European Champions in 1988. With those two playing up front, even Fred Olney couldn't have mismanaged Rumney down to their position at the bottom of the First Division of the South Hampshire League.

On the other hand, maybe he could. Swot wouldn't have put any disaster beyond the powers of Fred Olney.

"And if I *was* offside," George Watson went on as the van coughed into life with a gust of ozone-unfriendly black smoke, "which I wasn't, but if I was, then there's no way I was interfering with play, was there?"

"Well, I didn't think you were," agreed Swot. "Did you, Kev?"

"No," lied Kev. As far as he was concerned, George Watson had been interfering with play all afternoon. That was the only trouble with Swot. He just couldn't see how useless his dad was.

"Get that ball down from the tree did they, Mr Watson?" asked Kev as the van bumped out of the car park, its exhaust rattling.

Swot glared at his friend. At school Kev had a great knack of saying things which sounded innocent but which you just knew were really taking the mickey. Well, that was OK when he was trying it on with the teachers, but not when he was trying it with his dad.

"You got hold of that shot well," said Swot quickly. "Really well."

George Watson snorted. "Did you see the bounce I got? Did you?"

"No," said Kev.

"Bad, was it?" said Swot, although he couldn't say he'd seen the ball bounce badly either.

"Diabolical," said George Watson. "The thing bobbled just as I was going to hit it. I reckon I did well to get a shot in at all."

"Don't they roll the pitch, Mr Watson?" asked Kev. "You know, like they do for cricket?"

"Once a month," said George Watson over his shoulder.

"That's no good," said Swot angrily. "How can anyone play good football on a bumpy pitch?" Any half-decent manager would insist on a good playing surface for his team. As far as Swot was concerned, it was yet another black mark against Fred Olney.

"My granddad says they rolled the pitch every day at The Valley," said Kev.

Swot sighed. That was the other trouble with Kev. Every time he had the chance he would steer the conversation round to the fact that up until nine months ago he'd lived in the street next to The Valley, the famous ground used by Charlton Athletic in the days when they were the best team in London – days that could only be remembered by somebody the age of Kev's granddad, who had just happened to help work one of the turnstiles.

"Don't tell me," said Swot, "your granddad used to help push the roller."

"Right," said Kev. "Before breakfast."

Swot was getting irritated. "Pity your granddad didn't move to Rumney with you then, isn't it?"

"Just as well," said Kev. "Rumney haven't got a roller. Unless you count Jack Pettigrew's, that is."

"All right, you two," said George Watson, interrupting before the reference to Rumney's wealthy, Rolls-Royce-driving Chairman was able to spark off another round of argument. "Is this your turning, Kevin?"

Kev leaned forward and peered out of the side window. They'd reached the clutch of new houses which had sprung up on the outskirts of Rumney village over the past year or so.

"Yeah, this is me. Thanks, Mr Watson."

As Kev hopped out of the van's rear doors,

Swot wound down his window. "See you tomorrow, Kev," he said.

Arguments never got in the way of football. Every Sunday without fail, even if he and Kev had been at it hammer and tongs all week long, they would call a truce and meet for a kick-about at Rumney's small recreation ground.

"Usual time?" asked Swot. "Ten o'clock?"

Kev shook his head. "Have to be the afternoon, say ... two o'clock. I'm going to church in the morning. See ya."

And with that he was off, leaping up to head invisible footballs as he ran along the road towards his house.

Strange, thought Swot, as George Watson swung the van round and headed back towards the village. He'd never known Kev to go to Rumney's church before.

To the churchyard, yes, where Kev would treat the tombstones as imaginary defenders and dribble a ball round them with cries of "Wor, left him for dead!" but never to the church itself.

But then that was the one thing that was so predictable about Kev: he was completely unpredictable. Maybe that's why he's a Charlton Athletic supporter, thought Swot.

"Nearly time for the results," said George Watson. He clicked on the van's old radio.

The sound of the rattling exhaust pipe was drowned by the breezy introductory music to *Sports Report*.

"What do you think the headlines will be?" asked Swot. " 'Manchester United Hit Ten'?"

"I can tell you what they won't be," said George Watson.

" 'Rumney Require Roller'," said Swot with a half-smile.

"Close. How about 'Rumney Require New Manager'?"

Swot lost even the half-smile that he'd managed to summon up. "You're telling me! I tell you, Dad, Fred Olney hasn't got a clue."

"Fred Olney hasn't got a job now, either," said George Watson. "He's resigned. Rumney are on the look-out for a new manager."

# CHAPTER 3

## Kev Takes a Hand

Swot checked his watch again. A quarter past two. Where was he?

Kev almost always arrived first for their weekly kickabouts. Swot would turn the corner into Rumney Recreation Ground and there Kev would be, smacking a ball into the wire netting that surrounded the tennis courts and wheeling away as though he'd just scored the winner in the Cup Final.

Not today though. No sign of him.

Swot went back to practising banana shots, hitting the ball with the inside of his foot to make it swerve viciously in the air. At least that was the theory as outlined in the book he was currently reading, *Football The Brazilian Way*. Somehow it didn't seem to work for Swot. If anything his shots went straighter.

He was just wondering whether he'd turned over two pages and missed a bit about needing specially-shaped feet or a Brazilian in your family tree when Kev appeared on the far side of the Rec.

"At last!" he said.

The news about Fred Olney's resignation had just about driven him to bursting point. Swot had begun to feel like an over-inflated football waiting to be let down. And it looked as if he was going to have to wait for a few more minutes yet.

Kev seemed to be in no great hurry. He was positively dawdling, head down, across the Rec. At one point he bumped into the rope surrounding the cricket square and had to change route.

"What is he doing?" muttered Swot.

The question was only answered when Kev finally reached him. Kev was counting money.

"Two pounds forty-three," said Kev.

"He's resigned!" yelled Swot, unable to wait a moment longer.

Kev merely tutted. "Huh! And a couple of foreign coins."

"He's gone! Fred Olney has G-O-N-E gone!"

"I don't know. You can't trust anyone nowadays."

Swot stared hard at the other boy. He looked like Kev. Tracksuit trousers, latest line in trainers and a bright red football shirt with "Charlton Athletic" written across it – it had to be Kev. It was just that the Kev he remembered wasn't stone deaf.

He tried again. "Didn't you hear me?" he yelled. "He's resigned! Gone!"

"Who?" said Kev.

"Fred Olney!"

"Oh, right. Great."

"There's hope for Rumney yet! If we can get the right manager…"

He stopped. Kev was still studying the pile of coins in his hand.

"You don't seem very excited," said Swot.

"I am."

"Well, you don't look it."

"I am. Really," said Kev. "Two pound forty-three's not bad for the first time out."

Swot clapped a hand to his head. "What are you on about? And where did you get that money from?"

At last Kev showed some signs of having heard what had been said to him. "Church," he said. "You deaf or something? I told you I was going."

"You haven't pinched the Poor Box?"

"Car boot sale, stupid. In St. Winifred's car park. They have one every Sunday."

"You haven't got a car."

"No," said Kev, "but our Brian has." And with that he sat down and began to count his money again.

Swot gave in. Money, car boots – and now Kev's elder brother, Brian – had lost him completely. He removed all thought of banana-kicks and Fred Olney from his mind and sat down on his football.

"Explain," sighed Swot. "From the beginning."

"Me and Brian. . ." began Kev.

"Your brother Brian?" said Swot. He wanted to get this right first time.

"Correct. My brother Brian, who's just given me two pounds forty-three with loads more to come."

"Your elder brother Brian? The invisible Brian who stayed behind in London when you moved to Rumney last year..."

"Because he's at college studying electronics," nodded Kev. "But who's just come home because his course has finished, yes."

"The Brian who you reckon's never got any money? The Brian you reckoned used to write your parents begging postcards because they were cheaper than begging letters? That Brian?"

"The very same."

"So why has he just given you that money?" said Swot.

"It's a long story," warned Kev.

"It would be," sighed Swot. "Go on, then."

Kev took a deep breath. "Right, here goes. Our Brian was twenty-one last month and for his present the Wrinklies ... Mum and Dad," explained Kev as Swot gave him a blank look, "bought him a portable telly – y'know, to look at in the odd moments when he wasn't studying."

"You mean the electronics wizard hadn't

already made a television of his own?"

"No. But he *had* made himself a clock radio. That's what caused the trouble."

"What trouble?"

"The colour telly. It's bust. In bits."

"Hang on," said Swot. "You've lost me again. Let me get this straight. Your Brian makes a clock radio and ends up busting the telly your parents bought him for his birthday. Is that right?"

"Right."

"How come?"

Kev sighed as though he was a teacher dealing with a very thick pupil. "Because, dimbo, everybody's got a clock radio and Brian likes to be a bit different. So he decides to make a clock telly!"

"A clock telly," echoed Swot.

"Right," said Kev, as though clock televisions were the most natural device in the world. "So, not saying anything to the Wrinklies of course, our Brian takes the back off the telly, does a bit of jiggery-pokery inside to join it up to the clock radio, builds a nice shelf to put them both on and Bingo! One clock telly to wake him up in the morning! Give him his due, when it comes to electronics, he's a whizz."

"An electronics whizz doesn't go around blowing up his telly."

"Blow it up? Who said anything about it being blown up?"

"You said it was in bits."

"Not because he blew it up. Our Brian knows his stuff. It worked a treat."

"So what happened?" yelled Swot.

"He's no good at carpentry. The shelf fell down."

Swot's head was starting to feel as if it had been on the receiving end of one of Terry Potts' rocket shots. Worse was to come.

"So," he said slowly, "your Brian is selling things at car boot sales to get some money to buy a new telly. Have I got that right?"

"Right!" said Kev. "And giving me ten per cent of everything he makes. Twenty-four pound thirty today equals two pound forty-three for little old me."

"But *why?*" pleaded Swot.

"The price of my silence," said Kev. "I mean, if the Wrinklies were to find out about the telly..."

Swot was shocked. "You mean he's paying you to keep mum!"

"So that Mum don't find out. Or Dad. Right."

"But that's blackmail!" said Swot.

"That's business," said Kev. "Good money management, I call it."

It was the chance Swot had been waiting for – the chance to switch the conversation away from Kev's sordid schemes and back to the really important things of life.

"Good football management," he said. "That's what Rumney need."

"Too late," sniffed Kev. He gave a thumbs-down sign. "It's the big drop I reckon. Division Two here we come."

"Not if we win the last three games," said Swot. "A good manager could still save us."

"A good manager," scoffed Kev. "A good miracle-worker you mean."

"No, just a decent manager. That would be enough. I mean, anyone can see where Rumney are going wrong."

"Fred Olney couldn't."

"Well, I can. They're not fit, for a start. That's what I'd do first. Get them doing some circuit-training."

"Perhaps our Brian could be manager then," said Kev. "He could train them on circuits. And wiring, and soldering."

Swot treated the remark with the contempt it deserved and simply ignored it. "Then, I'd change their tactics."

"What, stay in the dressing room?" Kev hooted, throwing himself back on the grass. "At least that way they wouldn't get beat!"

"The defence is all over the shop," persevered Swot. But he was talking to himself. Kev's mind had drifted off into the world of car boot sales again.

"There must be loads of things at home we could get rid of," Kev muttered to himself. "I could make a fortune."

"Yes," said Swot, continuing his save-

Rumney catalogue. "I'd have to improve the defence first. It's leaking like a sieve."

"Possibly, possibly," said Kev.

"The flat back four system is useless. I'd definitely go for a sweeper."

"Sweeper?" muttered Kev, thoughtfully. "No, Mum'd miss that straight away. The sieve's not a bad idea though."

"That would release the full backs to support the front runners. A five-man midfield with instructions to close down the opposition quickly and break whenever they get the chance..." Swot was getting enthusiastic now. "...Magic! Total fluidity!"

Kev's eyes lit up. "The liquidizer! Great idea! She hasn't used that for years!"

"The only trouble is..."

"I couldn't get it up me jumper..."

That was it. Swot had heard enough. There they were, with Rumney Town facing its darkest hour, and all Kev could think about was money. He leapt to his feet, picked up the ball he had been squatting on and kicked it straight at Kev's head.

Kev moved quickly to the side. But, more by luck than design, Swot had managed to strike his best-ever banana shot. The ball swerved perfectly in the air and struck Kev beautifully on the ear before bouncing away towards the Rec's main entrance.

Swot raced after it, deciding as he ran that it was probably a good time to go home for an early tea.

Kev raced after Swot.

As races went, it was a no-contest. Kev was a big boy for his age and had a height and weight advantage. He was also a good runner, whereas Swot knew the theory about moving his legs fast but couldn't actually manage it in practice. He still had a long way to go to reach safety when Kev overtook him and grabbed him by the neck.

Swot braced himself for the avenging thump. Strangely, it didn't come. Instead he found himself being frog-marched out of the Rec and along the pavement to a telephone booth.

"Right," growled Kev as they reached it.

He pushed Swot inside, then began to thumb through the pages of the telephone directory.

"Parker, Peebles..." muttered Kev as he thumbed, "...Perkins, Petworth..." And then, "Got it!" He picked up the receiver, put one of his prized coins into the slot and punched in the number he'd found.

"What are you up to?" said Swot, still half-expecting some sort of a bashing.

"Rumney, Rumney, Rumney," Kev said angrily. "Get 'em fit. Bring in a sweeper. Rumney, Rumney, Rumney. That's all you can think about."

Swot heard a ringing sound. "Who are you calling?"

The ringing stopped with a click. "Hello," said a gruff voice.

Kev put his hand over the mouthpiece. "All right, clever dick," he said, "this is your big chance."

"Who's there?" hissed Swot.

"Hello," said the voice on the other end of the line. "Hello!"

Kev was holding the receiver towards him.

"Go on then, genius. Tell him you're available."

"What? Who?"

Kev pushed the telephone into Swot's hand with a nasty smile.

"Jack Pettigrew," he said. "Chairman of Rumney Town F. flippin' C. For you-hoo!"

# CHAPTER 4

## Calling Pettigrew

Swot was staring at the receiver as though it was a rattlesnake about to strike.

"Hello!" said a gruff voice again. "Pettigrew here. Who's there?"

"Go on, then," hissed Kev.

Swot struggled to make any noise at all. When he did, he sounded like a cat miaowing to be let out.

"Er..." he began. "Um..."

"Are you selling summat?" said Jack Pettigrew in his ear. "Because if you are I don't want any."

"No!" said Swot, suddenly finding his voice. Kev had grabbed him by the hair and was twisting it slowly. "No, I'm not selling summat ... er ... anything."

"So what d'you want then?"

"Er ... it's ...well ..."

"Well what?"

"Go on!" hissed Kev.

Swot was well and truly in a jam. As Kev gave another twist to his hair he realized he hadn't got much choice. Either he made a fool of himself with the Rumney Town Chairman or he ended up the only bald-headed fourth-former in school.

"I ... er ... the job!" he finally stammered.

"Job?" echoed Jack Pettigrew. "You mean t'manager's job?"

Swot nodded. Kev gave another twist.

"Er ... yes," said Swot. "The manager's job."

"Oh, aye," said Jack Pettigrew. "And what makes you think you could do it, eh?"

"Um. Well. I've seen all Rumney's games."

"So have I," growled Pettigrew, "but I haven't got a clue how to make 'em play any better."

"Go on, give him the theories," hissed Kev. "Flat back fours and all that stuff."

"W-w-well . . ." stammered Swot, "if the team had a more fluid organization. . ."

"Drown 'em you mean?"

"No, no, better tactical awareness, more movement off the ball. . ."

Pettigrew's voice crackled down the telephone line. "They do move off t'ball. Half of 'em don't see it more than half a dozen times from first whistle to last."

"Ah, but you see. . ." Swot was getting into his stride now. ". . .they aren't fit enough, Mr Pettigrew. I'd aim to increase their level of general fitness, that would have to be my number one priority. Constant movement needs high levels of fitness, you see. . ."

Jack Pettigrew coughed loudly. "Excuse me saying so," he said, "but you sound a bit on t'young side for a manager."

"Do I?" said Swot, then realized that he certainly did. He tried for a deeper voice, aiming somewhere between Popeye and Bluto. "I do?"

"Early twenties?" said Jack Pettigrew. "Am I close?"

"Close-ish," said Swot. He thought quickly. "Ah, but then you have to be able to get out there with the players, you see, Mr Pettigrew. Be a tracksuit manager. It's no good just giving the players instructions, you've got to be fit enough and young enough to show them what you mean."

A thoughtful silence came down the line. "True," said Jack Pettigrew eventually. "Fred Olney couldn't do it. He weren't fit. He got whacked out jumping up an' down on his cap."

"Did a lot of it though, didn't he?" muttered Kev.

"Ssshh!" sshhed Swot. Jack Pettigrew was speaking again. "Sorry, Mr Pettigrew, I didn't catch that."

"I said t'trouble is. . ."

"What?"

"I reckon you're too late."

"Definitely not!" insisted Swot. "Winning our last three games won't be easy, I'll give you that, but it can be done. Mr Pettigrew, let me tell you about some of the tactics I've got up my sleeve..."

"I mean, you're too late for the job," crackled Pettigrew.

Swot felt stunned. After finally getting around to saying he wanted the job it was a real blow to hear that it wasn't available any more.

"Oh," was all he could manage.

"One of t'players wants it, see? An' with the little bit left to the end of t'season, there don't seem much sense in doing owt else than bring in a caretaker."

Kev snorted quietly. "Undertaker, more like."

"So it's gone, then?" said Swot.

"Near enough. I'm seeing the player concerned tomorrow evening. Just to sort out t'details."

"Oh."

"Good of you to call though," said Pettigrew. "Mr ... what did you say your name was?"

"Er ... I didn't," said Swot. "It's..."

He stopped himself just in time. He could hardly say "Watson", could he? If he did, Jack Pettigrew might put two and two together and come up with his dad. That would be embarrassing.

"Mr?" repeated Jack Pettigrew.

Swot felt he had to say something. Next to him, Kev had finally let go of his hair. Now, as he looked around for inspiration he spotted the name on Kev's cherry-red football shirt.

"Er ... Charlton," said Swot. "Mr ... Charlton."

"Well, as I say, Mr Charlton," began Jack Pettigrew, "it was nice of you to..."

The line went silent, as though the Chairman had suffered some sort of blockage. Just as Swot had come to the conclusion that Pettigrew had left without saying goodbye, his voice returned. But it was a voice that had changed. It was different somehow, more of a whisper, as though he was in a cathedral.

"Charlton?"

"Er..." said Swot. "Yes."

Pettigrew sucked in his breath. "Not ... Charlton?"

"Ye-es," said Swot slowly, wondering where this was all leading.

"As in Bobby Charlton, Manchester United and England? And Jack Charlton, Leeds United and England, *and* manager of the Republic of Ireland? What I mean is..." said Pettigrew in hushed tones, "you're not ... y'know ... one of the family...?"

Swot suddenly realized why Jack Pettigrew's attitude had changed. He was wondering if a member of the famous Charlton dynasty had really called him on a Sunday afternoon to ask about being the manager of little Rumney Town F.C.! A fantastic thought flashed through Swot's mind. Could he say? No, of course he couldn't.

"No," said Swot. "I'm not one of the family."

"Pity," said Jack Pettigrew.

On the other hand, thought Swot, if it was the difference between getting his chance and missing it...

"But us Charltons are close, Mr Pettigrew. Very close."

It was true. Kev's Charlton Athletic football shirt was no more than a touch away. Swot was committed now.

"Us Charltons have got football in our blood, you know. When it comes down to it, we're really just one big football family. Bobby and Jack. And me..."

"There's football in your bit of t'family, is there?" said Jack Pettigrew.

"Oh, yes," said Swot truthfully, "there's football in our family all right. It's been there for ages."

"Ah see..." Swot could almost hear Jack Pettigrew thinking. "Right. Now look, er..."

"Jimmy," said Swot. "Jimmy Charlton."

"Jimmy," said Jack Pettigrew. "Right. Now, Jimmy. This has to be done proper. As I say, one of t'players is coming round here tomorrow evening and he deserves a fair hearing. It's t'least I can do ... before I give you the job, like. You're with me?"

"I'm with you."

"And . . . er . . ." Pettigrew gave a million-aire's cough, the sort that showed he wasn't going to part with more money than he had to. "There's nowt much I can afford by way of . . . y'know, payment. Rumney are a small club," he said with a self-conscious chuckle, "not Manchester United!"

Money? Swot hadn't considered money. He wasn't worried about money. "I don't want . . . ouch!" he began to say, before a fierce jab in the ribs stopped him in his tracks.

"How much?" hissed Kev.

"What?"

"Ask him how much," Kev repeated.

"Why?"

"Just ask him, noodle-head."

Jack Pettigrew helped out. "You don't want much, you say?"

"Er . . . yes . . . no."

The Rumney Chairman sounded pleased. "Well, that is gratifying, Jimmy. Most grati-fying. Would . . . er . . . fifty pounds a week be acceptable? One night's training and the game on Saturday. Just t'end of t'season, like."

"Er ... fine," said Swot, as Kev's head nodded up and down like a woodpecker drilling a tree.

"Grand!" said Jack Pettigrew. "Grand. Now look, we'd better do this right. Can you be round here tomorrow? Seven o'clock, say. I'll ask you a couple of questions, you give me the answers, we'll agree all the details and that'll be that. Right?"

Swot's mouth opened, but no sound came out. He'd been so carried away with the thought of directing Rumney's bid to save themselves from relegation that he just hadn't thought about the fact that he'd actually have to meet Jack Pettigrew. What had he done?! Suggested he was over twenty-one and a close relation of Bobby and Jack Charlton, that's what he'd done. Agreed expenses, that's what he'd done as well!

It was no good. He'd got to come clean. It had been all Kev's fault. Things had got out of hand. He would admit it, say he was sorry to have troubled him and that would be that.

"My place tomorrow then?" said Jack Pettigrew. "Seven sharp. Right?"

"Er ..." said Swot. "Now look ... Mr Pettigrew..."

And that was as far as he got. Before he could say he was sorry or anything like it the receiver was snatched from his hand.

"Right!" yelled Kev. "Seven tomorrow it is! Bye!" And as Swot looked on aghast he slammed the phone down.

Swot staggered out of the phone box. He couldn't have felt weaker at the knees if he'd just played two hours of extra time against Liverpool.

Behind him, Kev was grinning. "All right, Boss? The job's as good as yours."

Swot had gone pale. "What am I going to do?"

"What d'yer mean, what are you going to do?"

"What do you think I mean!" yelled Swot. "What do you think's going to happen tomorrow night?"

Kev grinned a little wider. "Tomorrow night," he said, "Jack Pettigrew, millionaire butcher and Chairman of Rumney Town F.C. is gonna get himself a new manager."

"You must be joking!" yelled Swot. "I'll tell you what Jack Pettigrew, millionaire butcher, is going to do! When he finds out he's been messed about by a fourteen-year-old schoolboy who's about as close a relative of

Bobby Charlton as our cat, millionaire butcher Jack Pettigrew is going to get hold of one of his meat cleavers and..."

"You'll be for the chop!" cackled Kev.

"It's not funny!"

Kev tried to look serious. "OK. You're right. It's not funny."

"What a mess," moaned Swot. "I'm done for."

"No, you're not. I've got a plan."

Swot went even paler. "And you know what you can do with your plan. You got me into this mess."

"Mess? What mess? The job's yours. No problem."

"'No problem', he says! I've told you, when I turn up..."

Kev held up a hand. "You are not gonna turn up."

"I'm not gonna turn up," echoed Swot. "But I am going to get the job." He shook his head in disbelief. "So how do you work that out?"

"Elementary, my dear Watson," said Kev.

"You are going to get the job *without* turning up."

"You must be mad!" yelled Swot. "You heard him. He wants to see me! You don't go around picking managers you haven't seen!"

"I didn't say he wasn't gonna see *somebody*. I said he wasn't gonna see *you*."

"Not going to see me..." said Swot.

"You a parrot or something?" said Kev. "Don't keep repeating everything I say. He's not gonna see you. He's gonna see somebody pretending to be you..."

"Pretending to be Jimmy Charlton..." said Swot.

"Right."

"Kev," said Swot patiently, "who is going to be stupid enough to do that?"

"Fifty pound a week, old Pettigrew said, didn't he?"

"Yes."

"Well, there you are then."

"There I am where then?"

Kev grinned, a wide toothy grin that stretched from ear to ear.

"Who do we know who's short of cash? New-telly-sized cash?"

Swot's mouth fell open. "Brian?"

"Brian."

"Your brother Brian?"

"Natch! It's perfect! Pettigrew doesn't know him. Nobody round here knows him. Did I tell you he'd grown a beard?"

Swot shook his head dumbly.

"Yeah, he has. Even I don't know if I know him half the time! So ... it's easy. Brian turns up saying he's Jimmy Charlton. You tell him about flat back fours and all that stuff, he trots it out for Pettigrew's benefit and Bingo! He gets the money, you get the glory." Kev looked at the amazed Swot. "What d'you reckon?"

"Brian?" said Swot. "Brian?" He gave an unhappy laugh, as though he'd just been told he was going to be executed, but not tomorrow. "He won't do it," he said.

"He will."

"Never."

"Believe me," said Kev. "He *will* do it."

# CHAPTER 5

## Bobby Who?

"I won't do it," said Brian Murrant.

"Brian..." pleaded Kev.

"No." Brian shook his head from side to side. "No, no, no."

"How d'you mean... 'No'?" said Kev.

"I mean N.O. As in not yes. No. Got it?"

Kev frowned. "You mean ... no? You won't do it?"

"What did I say?" said Swot.

"Hang on, hang on," said Kev. "Nothing's definite."

"Definitely no!" yelled Brian Murrant. "I will not pretend to be whoever it is you want me to be whenever it is you want me to pretend to be him. No!"

"Jimmy Charlton," said Kev. "Tomorrow night."

"NO!!"

"I think he means it," said Swot. His emotions were mixed. On the one hand he was pleased that he'd been right and Kev wrong – Brian couldn't be persuaded. But, at the same time, he felt pretty disappointed. As they'd walked from the Rec to Kev's house, he'd found himself planning training schemes and devising tactics. It would have been great to see his plans put into action ... Rumney Town saved from relegation...

The ever-persistent Kev tried again. "Think about the money, Brian," said Kev. "Three weeks left to the end of the season. Fifty pounds a week. That's a hundred-and-fifty. You could buy another telly and have a bit left over."

"No. I can make enough through the car boot sales. Without the danger of getting my head chopped off by a mad butcher."

Swot and Kev exchanged glances. Kev

shrugged. Swot thought for a moment it was a "What more can I do?" sort of shrug. He was wrong. It was a "Right-o, Brian, you've asked for it and you're going to get it" sort of shrug.

"Car boot sales are pretty dangerous, Brian," Kev purred.

A shadow crossed Brian Murrant's face. "How?"

"Well ... f'rinstance ... that nice new hat the Vicar's wife's walking about wearing..."

"What about it?"

"Well ... if our mum was to see her and think, 'Hey! I've got a hat like that' and come home and look for it..."

"You mean she didn't know? You said she gave it to you!"

"I did?" said Kev.

"Yes, you did!"

Kev looked blank. "No. I don't remember that."

Brian Murrant was looking worried. "What about the other things? That old ball gown?"

"She hasn't worn that for yonks. Don't worry about it."

"Don't worry about it!"

"There's no problem..." said Kev. "So long as she doesn't find out."

Brian Murrant glowered menacingly. "You'll be in it as well if she does," he growled. "You wouldn't escape."

"Ah," said Kev. "That's different."

"I thought it would be," said Brian.

"Yeah," said Kev. "Because then ... well ... I reckon the Wrinklies might find out about the telly as well, Brian."

"You wouldn't! We've got a deal. Ten per cent."

"But the car boots would have finished, wouldn't they? And they'd be bound to interrogate me. They're mean, those Wrinklies. They'd sit me in a chair and shine lights in me face and generally torture me."

"Come off it."

"But they might. And I'm allergic to pain, Brian. The sheer thought of it would make me crack. I ... I wouldn't be able to stop it slipping out..." *This* time he gave a "What can I do?" shrug. "If you get my drift."

Brian Murrant scowled at his younger brother. "I get your drift," he said. "But I'm still not doing it."

"Pity. A great pity." Kev shook his head, like a Godfather who'd had his final offer turned down and knew that now he was left with no alternative. "I thought we could have done business," he said.

"Look..." said Brian, "give me time to think about it, all right?"

Swot's hopes rose. He's weakening, thought Swot. It was time to add his weight to the attack. "We don't have time to play with, Brian. The interview with Jack Pettigrew is set for tomorrow."

Brian Murrant was starting to feel surrounded. "Give me until the morning, then. I'll tell you in the morning."

"Sorry," said Kev.

"We need an answer now, Brian," said Swot.

"Swot here's got plans to tell you about, see. You're gonna have to learn what to say. Get your act together and convince old man

Pettigrew you're worth the job."

"You could do it, Brian," said Swot, thinking that a bit of flattery might help. "I mean, you're intelligent."

"Def," agreed Kev.

"You look the part," said Swot.

"Do I?" said Brian.

Swot took in Brian's shoulder-length hair, and the new, stubbly beard. "Sure," he said, "you've got a footballer's appearance. In a Rumney tracksuit you'd look great."

"Yeah," said Kev. "Come on, what do you say?"

Brian took a deep breath. "If, just *if* I do it, you won't say anything about ... y'know ... the television."

Kev scratched his chin. "Television? What television?"

"So you'll do it?" said Swot.

"Er ... can I tell you in the morning?"

Kev looked dramatically at the clock. "What time do the Wrinklies get back?"

Brian Murrant cracked. He slumped into a chair. "All right! I'll do it!"

"Good man!" said Kev.

"Thanks, Brian," said Swot.

"So," said Brian Murrant, "who do I say I am?"

"Jimmy Charlton," said Swot briskly. "Got that? Jimmy Charlton. You're a distant relative of the one and only Bobby Charlton."

"Who?" said Brian.

# CHAPTER 6

## Are You Receiving Me?

It was Swot's turn to slump into a chair. "You don't know the first thing about football, do you, Brian?" he groaned.

The signs hadn't been good from the start, what with Brian Murrant being the only person in the world – apart, maybe, from the odd cave-dweller in the Himalayas – who hadn't heard of Bobby Charlton.

But things had got worse.

Now, an hour later, after being asked if it was the goalie who wore the face mask, how many points you got for a corner and a hundred-and-one other daft questions, Swot was ready to give up.

"You never asked me if I knew anything about football," said Brian Murrant. "All you wanted was somebody to go and see this Pettigrew bloke."

"Jack Pettigrew," breathed Swot.

He closed his eyes at the thought of it. Brian wouldn't last five minutes with him. The Rumney Chairman would eat Brian up and spit him out in pieces. "Let's forget it," he said.

Brian Murrant's face brightened immediately. "Forget it? Right! Fine!"

"Hang on, hang on," said Kev. "Don't be too hasty."

While Swot had been trying to teach his brother something – anything – about football, Kevin had been working out what ten per cent of fifty pounds a week for three weeks was. And now he had worked it out he didn't want to see it disappear.

He gave Brian a "Remember-me-and-what-I-know" look. "Try him again."

Brian nodded. "Go on, try me again," he sighed. "What's this side-off business all about?"

"Offside!" yelled Swot.

Kev started banging his head against the wall.

"It's no good," Swot said, "he'll never learn enough in time."

Kev stopped head-banging and sat down. "What we need is a bright idea."

"Such as?" said Swot irritably.

"I don't know!" yelled Kev. "Some way of you going in with him to tell him what to say ... like ... I don't know, saying you're his agent or something."

"Oh, very good," said Swot. "Very bright. 'Hello, Mr Pettigrew, this is Jimmy Charlton. I'm his agent, and I've come along to answer all your questions because poor old Jimmy here has lost his voice as well as his brains.'"

"It was only a suggestion," said Kev.

"And it couldn't have been much dumber. No, I tell a lie. It could. You could have suggested I stand outside Pettigrew's house and make signs at Brian through the window."

Kev's eyes lit up. "Hey! That's not a bad idea!"

"What!"

"No, I mean it! Thumbs-up could mean 'Yes, I'm confident we can do it, Mr Pettigrew...'"

"Do what? How do I get to hear the questions, stupid? Tune in to Radio 1?"

"On the radio..." It was Brian, and his voice had gone very quiet. Swot and Kev turned in unison to look at him.

"Brian?" said Swot.

Kev's brother didn't reply. He seemed to have gone into a trance.

"Brian," said Kev. "Are you receiving me? Over."

"Receiving you," murmured Brian Murrant, scratching his stubbly beard and looking glassy-eyed. "Over."

"Brian!" yelled Kev. "What are you on about?"

Kev's elder brother blinked and stood up. "It might work," he said to himself.

"Might work?" said Kev. "Might work? What might work?"

"Receiving you, receiving me," muttered

Brian. "In there with me. It might work."

"Eh?" But Brian wasn't there to answer. He had dashed up the stairs. The only noise they heard was a cry of "Ye-es!" as he reached the door of his bedroom.

"Hear that?" said Kev. "He went 'Ye-es!'."

"So?" said Swot wearily.

"He only goes 'Ye-es!' when he's got an idea. Come on!" Kev sprinted up the stairs and into his brother's room.

Swot followed wearily. He'd had enough ideas from the Murrant household to last him a lifetime. Slowly he trudged up the stairs. As he reached Brian's room he heard a tremendous clattering noise like bits of plastic, metal and assorted whatnots being tipped on to the floor.

He went through the door. There, sitting on the floor, a huge pile of plastic, metal and assorted whatnots in front of him, was Brian Murrant.

"Hold that," said Brian, pulling a small plastic box from the pile and handing it to Swot.

"What is it?"

"A hearing aid," said Brian. He continued sifting.

"Ah!" He pulled out a microphone and lead and gave it to Kev.

"Hey, I'm a pop singer!" cried Kev.

"Don't do that!" yelled Brian as Kev began to swing the microphone around. "That's the answer!"

"Answer?" said Swot.

"To how you can be in that interview with me!" yelled Brian. He was getting more and more excited now, diving in and out of the pile of junk on the floor, each time handing over something else.

"There!" he said finally. Kev and Swot looked at each other, then at the assorted bits and pieces they'd been given to hold. In addition to the microphone, Kev had ended up with a small printed circuit board and a container that looked like a metal sandwich box. Swot had the hearing aid, a portable radio, a batch of mysterious components and a handful of batteries.

"Where?" said Swot.

"There!" said Brian again. "I don't know why I didn't think of it sooner."

Kev winked in Swot's direction. "Told you, didn't I? The boy's magic."

"What is it all for, then?" asked Swot.

"Isn't it obvious?" said Brian.

"Course it is," said Kev.

Swot looked at Kev. "So what *is* it all for, then?"

"Er . . . you tell him, Bri."

"A simple two-way transmitter/receiver system," said Brian Murrant excitedly. "Not great, but good enough for the job in hand."

"A two-way radio? Like the police have?"

"Same idea," said Brian. "But much simpler. Look. . ."

He took the various bits they were holding and laid them out on his bed. "Hearing aid. Normal function: to pick up noises. . ."

"Like Jack Pettigrew," said Kev, "who's the biggest noise round here."

"To pick up noises," repeated Brian, "and send them to the earpiece." He tapped the plastic blob linked to the hearing-aid box.

Swot was ahead of him. "But if those noises were to be sent to somewhere else. . ."

"Such as this loudspeaker," continued Brian, "and the loudspeaker is with you. . ."

"Then Swot'll hear old Pettigrew's questions!" Kev was ecstatic. "Told you he was a genius, didn't I?"

"But," said Swot, "hearing Jack Pettigrew's questions is only half of it. How do I get the answers back to you?"

Kev saw that part of the answer immediately. "The microphone!"

"A tricky bit of micro-electronics," said Brian Murrant thoughtfully. "The hearing-aid box will need a receiver in it, and a bit of work to connect it up so that what you say comes out in the earpiece, but . . . it should be possible."

"Should?" said Kev menacingly. "Only should?"

"All right. Will," said Brian.


They retired downstairs to the kitchen and left Brian to it.

Swot spent the next two hours making notes and preparing for the big interview. Kev spent the time counting his money and occasionally disappearing upstairs to check on Brian's progress.

"Any news?" Swot asked as Kev returned from his zillionth visit to Brian's inner sanctum.

Until now Kev's reply had been boringly consistent. "He says it's coming along, coming along," and Swot had wondered, with equal consistency, if Brian was up in his room trying to make a bus. But this time was different.

Kev returned to the kitchen slowly. When he spoke, it was in a voice full of awe, like an announcer telling the nation that Liverpool had lost to Crewe Alexandra Reserves. "He wants you to go up. Just you. Now."

Swot leapt to his feet and dashed up the stairs. Brian Murrant met him at the door of his room. "Notice anything?" he said.

"No, Brian," said Swot, wondering why he was being asked such a stupid question, "you still look pretty much the same as you did two hours ago."

"Good. That means you didn't spot this." He lifted his long hair away to reveal the hearing aid's plastic blob of an earpiece stuck in his right ear, a thin wire trailing away from it and down the back of his neck.

"No, I didn't," said Swot, who hadn't. "Where's the rest of it?"

"Here." Brian Murrant lifted his jumper to reveal the small hearing-aid case clipped on to his belt.

"Neat," said Swot. "Where are the other bits?"

Brian motioned him into his room. There on the table, in a specially-cleared space amongst the clutter, stood three items: the microphone, the loudspeaker and, in between both, the metal sandwich box. The microphone and the loudspeaker didn't look any different, but the metal box certainly did. It now had an aerial poking skywards from its back and a couple of knobs plus a red light on the front.

"You sit there," commanded Brian.

Swot sat down in front of the microphone. "Now what?"

"Give me half a minute to get downstairs. Then turn that left–hand knob."

"Is that all?"

"You'll see," said Brian, as he closed the door. Moments later, Swot heard him hopping down the stairs. He counted slowly to thirty. Did another five for luck. Then he turned the left-hand knob.

Things started happening. The little red light came on. The loudspeaker made a loud crackling noise which slowly faded. And then, amazingly, into the room came the unmistakable voice of Kev.

"What d'yer mean, ask you a question?"

"Don't argue. Just ask me a question." It was Brian.

"All right. Why are you such a plonker?"

"A football question."

Silence. Then the excited voice of Kev as he realized what was going on. "Hey! It's a test, innit? You're testing! Er ... think of a question ... er ... me mind's gone blank!"

"Give you a pound if you think of one I can't answer," said Brian.

"Right! Who won the F.A. Cup in 1964? And who did they beat?"

Silence again. Swot checked the red light. It was still on. Why wasn't there any noise?

"Er…" said Brian through the loudspeaker. "Er…"

Of course! It's my turn to speak, realized Swot.

He leaned towards the microphone. "West Ham United," he said clearly. "They beat Preston North End. The score was 3–2. And the winner was scored by Ronnie Boyce." He added for good measure, "Did you get all that, Brian? Over and out."

He got his answer immediately, as Brian Murrant's voice came crackling through the loudspeaker again. "In response to your question, Kevin, West Ham United won the F.A. Cup in 1964, beating Preston North End by 3 goals to 2. Oh, yes! And the winner was scored by Ronnie Boyce."

Swot leapt in the air. It worked! It really worked!

Jack Pettigrew, here we come!

# CHAPTER 7

## At Pettigrew's Place

Swot weighed out the final consignment of Golden Delicious and tipped them hurriedly into a brown paper bag. "Finished, Mrs Young!" he yelled.

"OK, dear," said the woman who helped out in the shop every evening. "You get off. I'll lock up."

Swot didn't need telling twice. He charged outside and hared along the road. Why tonight? he asked himself. Everything had been going swimmingly. He'd worked out the schedule, and taken Kev through it at length. They'd even missed out on the Big Match in the playground to get it right.

5.45 Finish homework – or leave it.

5.46 Do a final thirty minutes preparation for any trick questions Jack Pettigrew might have up his sleeve.

6.16 Leave home.

6.25 Rendezvous with Kev and Brian at Rec.

6.30 Drive to Jack Pettigrew's place in Brian's car.

6.40 Arrive at Jack Pettigrew's place.

6.45 Find somewhere quiet to park (e.g. round the back).

6.46 Connect up equipment.

6.50 Connect up Brian.

6.55 Brian sneaks round the front way.

7.00 Brian knocks at front door.

7.00 + 10 secs. Jack Pettigrew says "Howdo, Jimmy?" or something like that.

7.00 + 20 secs. Brian alias Jimmy Charlton goes inside.

7.01 Start of interview.

7.30 End of interview.

7.31 Rumney have new manager!

Swot was fuming. Everything had been going to plan until his dad had come along and fouled things up.

By 5.45 he'd finished his homework.

By 6.13 he'd covered ten sheets of paper with answers to questions Jack Pettigrew might have up his sleeve, trouser leg, or anywhere else for that matter, and attached them to a clipboard.

And then, at 6.14, just as he was getting ready to leave, the plan had been altered for him...

6.14    Dad sticks head round door, wearing his best suit. He says, "Got to go out, Son. Help Mrs Young with tomorrow's orders, there's a good lad."

6.15    Dad leaves front door of his little shop. Gets into van marked, "George Watson, Greengrocer". Drives off.

6.16    S. Watson starts packing bags like a lunatic.

6.29  S. Watson finishes, yells "Finished, Mrs Young".

6.30  S. Watson belts down the road towards Rumney Rec.

6.40  S. Watson arrives fifteen minutes late to withering look and loads of abuse from K. Murrant.

"Come on!" yelled Kev, leaning out of the window of Brian Murrant's car. "Can't you go any faster'n that?"

"Had to help with some packing up," gasped Swot as he staggered into range.

"Sounds like you're the one who's packing up," said Kev. "Come on, get in. We're late."

Swot opened a rusty rear door and flopped exhausted into the back seat, leaning heavily on a large brown holdall. "Hey, watch it!" cried Brian from the driver's seat.

Kev turned round. "Our UNCLE's in there!"

Swot's brain struggled with what he'd just heard. Maybe it was a classic case of oxygen starvation after running too far, too fast. Had he really heard what he thought he'd heard? "In here?" he said, recoiling from the holdall. "Your uncle's in here?"

Surely Kev wasn't selling parts of his relatives as well now?

"UNCLE, dimbo!"

"It's short for UNdetectable Communicating and Listening Equipment," said Brian.

Swot unzipped the holdall. Inside he saw the jumble of wires and equipment which made up Brian Murrant's invention.

"Is it all right?" asked Brian Murrant. "It wasn't built to withstand vibratory influences."

"Eh?"

"It weren't designed so berks like you could sit on it," said Kev, who was obviously fluent in Brian's electronics-speak.

Swot checked the bits. To his relief, nothing seemed damaged. "Looks OK," he said.

"Good," said Brian. "This is an important test."

Good? thought Swot. Brian Murrant almost sounded keen. More than that. He *did* sound keen. Certainly a lot keener than he would have felt if somebody had been black-mailing him into facing a dangerous Jack Pettigrew. Swot gave Kev a quizzical look.

"Brian's been thinking. He reckons he's on to something with UNCLE," said Kev. "It all depends on tonight. If it works ... man, the market's wide open! Secret Service, Special Branch, James Bond ... he can sell the design anywhere. We could make millions!"

Swot allowed himself a smile. So, the victim wanted to go through with it as well! Things were working out fine.

"Then it's next stop Jack Pettigrew," he said. "Let's go."

Unlike George Watson (greengrocer), Jack Pettigrew (butcher) didn't live above any of the thirty-two shops he owned. He lived in a large house on the outskirts of Rumney village.

The imposing front of Jack Pettigrew's house faced on to the main Rumney Road. Most visitors to the house would turn right, pass under a decorative archway designed in the form of two pork chops leaning against each other, and continue on up the gravel driveway until they reached the house.

But Brian, Kev and Swot did no such thing. Their car continued on past the entrance for another fifty metres, then turned right into a narrow lane.

"Right again," said Swot as they approached another tiny turning.

Brian Murrant's car swung into the narrow opening.

"And stop." Swot looked out of the car's rear window. Through the trees the back of Jack Pettigrew's house was just visible.

"Will UNCLE work from here? It's not out of range?"

Brian Murrant shook his head. "Should be fine," he said. "So long as that house hasn't got lead-lined walls you'll hear me as clear as a bell."

"Talking of which," said Swot, checking his clipboard, "you should be ringing Jack Pettigrew's bell in..." he checked his watch, "eight minutes time. So come on then."

Five minutes later, fully wired up, Brian Murrant was retracing their route round to the front of the house.

Kev had moved across to the driver's seat of Brian's car. He was holding the UNCLE controls, his finger toying nervously with the ON/OFF knob on the front. Swot, who had moved forward to the passenger seat, was holding the UNCLE microphone. Behind them, on the back seat, sat the loudspeaker.

"Switching on..." said Kev in a mission-control voice, "now!" He clicked the knob to ON.

Swot leaned forward. "Control to Jimmy. Control to Jimmy. Are you receiving me?"

Brian's voice came through the loudspeaker at once. "Jimmy here," it said. "I've turned into the drive." They heard a different crackling noise from the one the loudspeaker usually made. The sound of gravel being scrunched, Swot realized.

"Receiving you loud and clear, Jimmy."

"Now I'm coming up to the front door. I'm ringing the bell."

In the car, Swot and Kev held their breath as they heard the sound of a door being opened. The loudspeaker hissed and crackled. Then they heard Jack Pettigrew's voice.

"Jimmy Charlton, is it?! Hey! Grand to meet thee, lad! Come in!"

"Thanks, Mr Pettigrew," they heard Brian say.

Then they heard the door close. The interview was about to begin.

# CHAPTER 8

## Reet, Jimmy!

"Sit yourself down, Jimmy," said Jack Pettigrew.

"Coming through loud and clear, ain't he?" said Kev.

Swot nodded. He gripped the microphone a little tighter. "Well, let's hope I'm coming through just as loud and clear at his end."

"I must say, Jimmy," Jack Pettigrew crackled out of the speaker, "I had no idea you were in't crowd watching our little team. I 'spect you've worked out by now we're not quite oop t'Manchester United standard. Eh?"

"Er ... well," began Brian.

"Say something, then!" hissed Kev in Swot's ear.

Swot turned to the microphone. "Brian!" he said into it. "Brian! Tell him: no, but they've got a lot of promise."

The loudspeaker crackled again. Swot's heart leapt as Brian Murrant's voice came through. "No. But they've got a lot of promise, Mr Pettigrew."

"Yeahh!" crowed Kev. "He must be getting us!"

Swot waved at him to be quiet. A crowing

Kev was no aid to concentration. "Brian," he said into the microphone. "Tell him: if they had a manager who could bring the best out of them they'd be pretty good."

"If they had a manager who could bring the best out of them," echoed Brian Murrant, "they'd be pretty good. Very good, in fact."

"A manager like you, eh Jimmy?"

"Agree with him!" hissed Swot.

"Yes, Mr Pettigrew."

"Call me Jack."

"Yes, er . . . Jack. A manager like me."

The loudspeaker crackled with the sounds of somebody getting up and beginning to walk about.

"Well now, Jimmy. I'll be straight with ye. I've just spoken to the other lad – the Rumney player I told you about on't phone – and he gave a good account of hi'self. But. . ." the footsteps stopped ". . .having a Charlton as manager of my team is a great attraction."

"Tell him you're only a distant relative," urged Swot.

"I'm only a distant relative," they heard

Brian Murrant say. "Eighth cousin. Fifteen removed."

"All right, there's no need to go overboard!" yelled Swot.

"Aye," said Jack Pettigrew, "but a Charlton's a Charlton. I mean, some of t'magic must rub off, I reckon."

"Nice of you to say so, Jack," said Brian.

"However. Happens I'm a believer in doing things fair and above board. So, Jimmy – what's your thinking for Rumney? Can you do it? Can you pull us out of t'fire and keep us in't First Division?"

"I think so, Jack," said Brian after Swot had told him to.

"Good, good," crackled Jack Pettigrew through the loudspeaker. "And how d'you reckon you can do that?"

"Well..." began Swot.

"Well..." began Brian.

"Circuit training, Jack," said Swot. "Start them with a good spell of circuit training, that's what I'd do."

Back bounced Brian Murrant's voice.

"Circuit training, Jack. I'd start them with circuit training."

"Aye. What sort of circuit training. . ."

And that, in the middle of Jack Pettigrew's first tricky question, was when the loud-speaker went dead.

Brian Murrant coughed.

He coughed again.

On the far side of the room, Jack Pettigrew waited.

Brian Murrant clutched at his ear and started wiggling the hearing aid's plastic blob around.

"Summat wrong with tha's ear, Jimmy?" said Pettigrew.

"No!" said Brian Murrant, taking his hand away fast. "No, no. Nothing. Just can't believe I'm ear, Jack! Ha–ha!"

"Eh?" said the Rumney Chairman.

"Joke!" said Brian. "Just a joke!"

"Ah," said Jack Pettigrew.

Starting to panic, Brian tapped at the

hearing-aid unit underneath his jumper.

"Summat wrong with tha's stomach, then?" Jack Pettigrew asked.

"No!" squeaked Brian. "Just ... er ... a bit of indigestion! Yes!"

He began to babble wildly, anything to waste a bit of time. "Must have been the sausages I had for tea. Horrible they were. Evil. Ugh! Can't stand sausages. Or chicken. Or bacon. Maybe all meat disagrees with me. Think I'll become a vegetarian..."

"Ah see," said the wealthy butcher. But it was clear from the look in his eye that he didn't. "So what sort of circuit training were you thinking of for t'Rumney lads? Eh? *Mister* Charlton?"

Brian Murrant's car was the scene of a lot of panic too.

"There must be a wire loose!" yelled Kev.

"A screw loose, more like it," screamed Swot. "In your Brian's head! This lot's supposed to work!"

"It did!"

Swot waggled the microphone under his nose. "Well, it doesn't now!"

"Battery!" yelled Kev. "The battery must have gone flat! Maybe there's another one in the bag."

He began scrabbling in the holdall, only to emerge a few moments later. "There isn't."

Swot thought about what to do next. Should he scream? Should he rush off and throw himself under the next bus that came along? What?

He did neither of these things. In his frustration he simply grabbed his clipboard and gave the UNCLE control unit an almighty thump.

Back in the house, Brian Murrant was struggling.

"Circuit training," he said. "You're asking me what sort of circuit training I'd give them?"

"Aye," said Jack Pettigrew bleakly.

"Well ... er ... it would be ... er ... training..."

"Aye, I reckoned on that."

"Er ... in circuits."

"That all?"

"No. Oh, no!" Brian Murrant racked his brain. "Er ... they'd ... er ... go round and round. Yes, definitely. I'd say they'd go round and round."

"Round what?"

"A circuit."

"Doing what?" growled Jack Pettigrew. "Getting dizzy?"

Then Brian gave an enormous sigh. "Doing squat-jumps to build up their thigh muscles for speed off the mark, press-ups to increase upper-body power and lung capacity, trunk curls to strengthen back muscles and working with weights to increase their overall fitness."

Jack Pettigrew's mouth fell open. "Aye," he said eventually, "that sounds all reet, Jimmy. Tell us more."

\* \* \*

In the passenger seat of Brian Murrant's car, Swot gave a big sigh of relief, too. Whacking the UNCLE system with his clipboard had had a magic effect. The thing had burst back into life again.

"No harm done," said Kev, as they heard Brian repeating Swot's circuit training answer.

"Except to my nerves," muttered Swot.

"Good practice for being a manager then, ain't it?" said Kev, unsympathetically.

Jack Pettigrew's voice crackled over the speaker. "That sounds all reet, Jimmy. Tell us more."

Kev gave Swot a nudge in the ribs. "Go on, then. Tell him more."

Swot leaned into the UNCLE microphone and did just that. He made suggestions about practising set-pieces. Then, after consulting his clipboard while Brian Murrant was repeating what he'd said, he told him about how Rumney needed to use the width of the pitch to stretch the opposition.

How they could hit the opposition on the break.

How they could change their tactical formation to employ a floating midfield with zone markers.

Twenty minutes later he said, "Brian – ask him if he'd like to hear about my own variation on the offside trap."

"Then there's my own variation on the offside trap, Jack. Would you like to hear about that?"

"No, Jimmy," they heard Jack Pettigrew say. He sounded thoughtful even through the crackle of the loudspeaker. "I found all that very impressive. Very impressive indeed."

The speaker fell silent, as though Jack Pettigrew was building up for the $64,000 question. He was. Over the air it came.

"But will it keep us oop, Jimmy lad? Save us from t'big drop into Division Two?"

Swot spoke crisply into the microphone. "I have every confidence that, at the end of the day, it will," he said in his best football-speak.

"I have every confidence that, at the end of the day, it will," echoed Brian.

Silence again. But only for a moment. Then, the voice of Jack Pettigrew crackled through. "Reet, lad. You've got t'job. Good luck, and if you can keep Rumney oop you'll be a ruddy hero."

In the car, pandemonium broke out. Kev began a sitting-down tap-dance.

Swot yelled "Wahoo!!" and then, remembering the effect he'd had on Brian's eardrum the last time he yelled into the microphone he threw his arms round Kev.

Only a sudden noise from the loudspeaker

stopped the celebration. "Ah'd better have a word with t'other applicant," Jack Pettigrew was saying, "Tell him the bad news. You hang on there, Jimmy, and I'll bring him in to meet thee. He's one of your players, after all."

Footsteps, followed by the opening of a door, came from the loudspeaker. A short pause and then they heard the door open again, this time followed by the sound of two pairs of footsteps.

Then Jack Pettigrew's voice.

"Jimmy here's your new manager."

"How do, Jimmy," said a third voice. For some reason, Swot thought it sounded familiar.

"I wanted the manager's job," said the voice, "but you got it. Fair enough. I'll be right behind you. You can rely on me."

"Thanks very much," said Brian. "Er..."

"Eh, I haven't done t'introductions," said Pettigrew. "Jimmy Charlton. This was your challenger for t'manager's job. George Watson."

In the car, Swot and Kev just looked at each

other. It was Kev who broke the silence. "Your dad," he said simply.

"My dad," echoed Swot.

Kev gave a little laugh. Then a bigger one. Then he simply cracked up and laughed until the tears ran down his cheeks.

"Your own dad," he gurgled, "you've just beat your own dad!"

So that's where he was going earlier on, thought Swot. That's why he was wearing his best suit!

"He didn't say," he muttered. "Why didn't he say?"

"Don't matter now, man," said Kev. "You beat him fair and square."

"I suppose you're right."

"Course I'm right," said Kev. He had disconnected the loudspeaker and was packing it away.

Thoughtfully, Swot unplugged the microphone from the UNCLE base unit and began to pack them in the holdall. Yes, maybe Kev was right.

"So what's yer plan for tomorrow, then?"

said Kev, adding with a broad grin, "Eh, Boss?"

Swot was still miles away. "Tomorrow?" he said.

"Tomorrow," repeated Kev. "Today, Monday. Tomorrow, Tuesday. Right? Rumney's training night."

Training! In the excitement and confusion it had slipped his mind completely! There was no time to lose. He had schedules to work out, plans to devise, free-kick strategies to formulate.

Kev was right. Football was a hard game, a game of winners and losers. And in this case George Watson, his own dad, had been a loser. He'd beaten him fair and square.

"You got some ideas, then?" said Kev.

"Plenty," said Swot, grim-faced. "Rumney are going to find out what training *really* means."

# CHAPTER 9

## Plan 4B

The door to the Rumney changing room swung open slowly. In trooped a group of men, each looking as though they'd been put through a mangle.

"Eh, my aching legs," groaned Norman Adlam, collapsing on to the nearest bench. "Jimmy Charlton's going to be the death of me, I know he is!"

"Legs? You want to have my back!" Rob "Corky" Corcoran, the Rumney goalkeeper, winced in agony. "I must have done a billion sit-ups out there!" He sat down slowly. "I said to him, 'What's it all about?' I said."

"And what did he say?"

"He put his hand to his ear," said Corky Corcoran, miming the action, "and then he says, 'it'll keep you flexible', he says."

"He did the same to me," said Norman Adlam.

"What, made you do a billion sit-ups?"

"No, put his hand to his ear. Y'know, when I conked out after all those sprints and he came over and told me I'd feel the benefit on Saturday. Peculiar habit, eh?"

"What, sprinting? You can say that again."

"Berk! Putting his hand to his ear, I mean."

Terry Potts clomped into the changing room. He snatched up a cup of tea in his huge police-sergeant's hands. "Phew! That was a training session and a half," he gasped. "Feels like I've been on the beat for a week non-stop."

Norman Adlam rested his head against the changing-room wall. "I won't make it to the end of the season," he croaked. "Jimmy Charlton's going to finish me off before then."

"And me," said Corky Corcoran.

"Even the young 'uns found it hard going,"

said Terry Potts. "I saw Baz Lucas crawl into the dugout when we were doing those sprints."

"Was that the first thousand or the second thousand?" wheezed Norman Adlam.

Terry Potts went on, "And if the young 'uns found it tough, what it did to old George is anybody's guess."

The three players looked at each other.

"Talking of George..." said Corky Corcoran.

Norman Adlam finished the sentence for him. "Where is he?"

The question was soon answered. "Here," said a voice.

They looked round. Framed in the doorway was George Watson. His face was white and his mouth hanging open. His eyes were staring straight ahead, unblinking.

"George!" said Norman Adlam. "How you feeling, mate?"

"Hard work, eh George?" said Terry Potts.

George Watson's mouth moved slowly up and down. His head moved slowly from side to side. "No problem, lads," he said as he fell on the floor.

"You don't reckon twenty laps of the pitch was a bit too much, then?" said Kev.

They were huddled in the back of Brian Murrant's car, parked in what used to be Fred Olney's spot. It was an ideal spot, alongside the touchline and giving a good view of the whole pitch, but not too close to the dugout.

Swot shook his head. "Nope," he said, explaining. "Stamina, Kev. That's what it's all about. Skill allied to speed and stamina. That's what your top teams have. Look at Liverpool. They're still going strong after ninety minutes."

The UNCLE loudspeaker crackled. "Well, the Rumney players didn't look too strong a minute ago, young Swot," said Brian.

Swot looked out through the car's windscreen to where Kev's brother, seemingly talking to himself, was standing outside the changing rooms.

"Especially your dad," continued Brian. "I reckon he was on his last legs."

"No, he was OK," said Swot, hoping he sounded more confident than he felt.

"He looked pretty rocky to me," said Kev. "I mean, he's no spring chicken, is he?"

"It was the sprinting that did him a mischief," crackled Brian. "They were all moaning about that."

"Speed off the mark," said Swot, without sympathy. "It's the only way they'll be first to the ball."

"Got to win it to use it," said Kev, echoing another of Swot's favourite sayings.

"But you had 'em doing short sprints, long-sprints, backwards sprinting and sprinting in zig-zags!"

"Different muscle groupings," said Swot. "Footballers don't run in straight lines, you know."

"Well," said Brian, "some of them can't even walk in straight lines now." Out on the pitch, they saw Kev's brother look at his watch. "I gave them ten minutes break like you said. They'll be out again soon. Maybe."

"What next, then?" said Kev.

Swot checked the list on his clipboard. They'd done the stamina work. They'd done the speed work. "Skills exercises," he announced into the microphone. "Twenty minutes dribbling around cones, then another twenty playing two-touch."

"That all?" said Brian.

"No," said Swot referring to his clipboard again. "Then finish off with the free-kick practice I told you about." He checked his chart, all squiggles and arrows. "Plan B4. And," he said sternly, "keep them going until they get it right!"


"Go!" hissed Swot into the UNCLE microphone.

"Go!" yelled Brian Murrant, out on the Rumney pitch.

On the edge of the penalty area the little huddle of players broke up as each of them started to sprint off in different directions.

Baz Lucas ran towards the penalty spot. Marco "Polo" Pirelli sprinted to the near post. Keith Burwood ran off towards the far post.

"George!"

As his new manager shouted at him, George Watson found a last little burst of energy and ran away in the direction of the corner flag. They must have tried this free kick strategy thirty times now and he still couldn't get the hang of it. Running away from the ball, he thought. It's not natural.

But, as Jimmy Charlton yelled at him from the touchline, he did it.

From twenty metres outside the penalty box, Terry Potts strode up to the ball. He floated it gently into the penalty area, now rapidly emptying as players ran off at all angles. Only one was actually looking at the ball – "and that's the beauty of it," the new manager had explained, with his hand to his ear.

Funny mannerism, thought Terry Potts. To go with some of his funny ideas. Or were they funny ideas? Watching as his free kick floated into the area, Terry Potts saw the defenders run with the players they were marking.

He saw a gap open up.

And then he saw, for the first time in thirty goes, gangly Norman Adlam stride into that gap, totally unmarked, to plant a firm header beyond Corky Corcoran and into the back of the net.

"Yeah!! It worked!!" hollered Terry Potts.

"Wa-hay!" echoed the other players.

Even Corky Corcoran looked appreciative – and glad that it was only a training session.

"Well done, lads!" called Brian Murrant, five seconds after Swot had told him to. "Let's call it a day."

"Good one, eh?" said Norman Adlam to Terry Potts as they left the pitch. "I can see what he's on about now."

"Took you long enough," said Terry Potts, slapping him on the back.

"It was George here," said Norman Adlam. "He kept trying to beat me to the ball."

"Well," muttered George Watson behind them, "running away from the ball. It's not natural."

"Still, at least we got it in the end," said Norman Adlam. "I thought we were going to be here all night."

"So did I," said Terry Potts. "And the lads down at the station wouldn't have liked that one little bit."

"Why's that, Pottsie?" laughed Norman Adlam. "Get worried if their sargie-wargie is latie-watie, do they?"

"Too right," growled the police sergeant. He nodded to where, over on the far side of the ground, a car with a red-white-and-blue strip light on its roof was pulling into the car park. "Because it means he's missed his liftie-wiftie and he gets really miserable when that happens. But as it is, Normie," said Terry Potts breaking into a trot, "you did it just in time. See you on Saturday, lads."

"All right, Sarge?" said PC Roland Cape, with

a grin. In his rear-view mirror he could see Terry Potts changing into his Sergeant's uniform in the back of the panda car.

"Not so bad," said Potts.

"Survived, then?"

"Looks like it, don't it?"

"Thought you might be a bit tired, like. Taking all of them free kicks."

"It did go on a bit," said Potts. Not unlike you, Roland, he thought.

"Got it right in the end, though. Plan B4, weren't it?"

Terry Potts looked at the back of Roland Cape's neck. He'd often wondered if driving a panda car around too much softened your brain, and Cape was living evidence that it might well be so.

"Roland, what are you on about?"

"Using an electric hailer or summat was he, Sarge? Your manager?"

"Why?"

"Just thought I picked him up on the car radio as I got near the ground, that's all. Chuntering on about plan B4 or summat."

"Roland," said Terry Potts, doing up his blue tie.

"Yes, Sarge?"

"Do us a favour."

"What, Sarge?"

"Belt up."

"Yes, Sarge."

In another back of another car – Brian Murrant's – Swot was feeling well satisfied as he and Kev packed the UNCLE equipment into its holdall. For one thing, Rumney Town had done some serious fitness work – a lot more than they'd ever done with Fred Olney, who thought a dozen press-ups was asking too much. And for another, they now had a surprise weapon – a free kick tactic the players knew like the back of their hands.

Waiting until George Watson had staggered off the pitch and was safely out of sight in the Rumney changing room, Swot and Kev clambered out of Brian's car and ambled across to the Watson van.

"UNCLE worked beautifully," Swot said.

"Magic," agreed Kev. "No hiccups tonight."

"Brian'll be pleased."

"You bet. He'll have James Bond wanting one next."

"Yes," repeated Swot, "he'll be really pleased."

And so it came as some surprise to him that, when Brian Murrant came off the pitch, he looked anything but pleased.

Quite the opposite. He was looking pale. Almost as pale, thought Swot, as the Rumney's players had looked after their circuit training.

"That ... er..." said Brian, trying to look unconcerned, "...police ... er, y'know ... police ... er ... car. What ... er ... want anything, did it?"

"Terry Potts," said Kev quickly. "He's a wanted man."

"He is? Oh. Good."

"Terry Potts is a policeman," explained Swot. "Sometimes he gets a lift to the station straight from training."

"Ah," said Brian. He gave a weak smile. "Why?"

"Nothing. Nothing. Thought he'd been arrested. Ha-ha. Good. That's all right, then," he said as he walked away.

Swot slipped into the passenger seat of the van to wait. Ten minutes later, after an exhausted George Watson had eased himself into the driver's seat with a groan, they were on the way home.

Swot began to dream of victory in Saturday's match. And he quickly forgot that when Brian Murrant had said "That's all right, then," the look on his face had said that it certainly wasn't all right.

# CHAPTER 10

## Theory and Practice

Saturday arrived at last.

After the successful use of UNCLE at Tuesday's training session, Swot had waited for match day to arrive with growing impatience.

School had been a bind. Homework had been something he just hadn't been able to concentrate on. But now the big day was here.

"Right, then?" said George Watson as they left Mrs Young in charge of the shop and set off for the Rumney ground. "I reckon we're gonna win today."

"I think so too," said Swot.

"So long as that new manager of ours

doesn't try too many of his fancy ideas on us."

"Fancy ideas?" said Swot, trying not to sound too hurt. "What fancy ideas?"

"All that free kick stuff he was giving us Tuesday night, fr'instance. Load of rubbish."

"It worked though, didn't it? Looked good from where I was ... sitting in the van," he added hastily.

"Practice is practice," growled George Watson. "Matches are different."

"I don't see why."

"Because you only get one go in a match, Son, that's why. The ref doesn't say, 'Oh dear, lads, you missed. Never mind, have another go and see if you score this time.' Does he now?"

"Of course not," said Swot. "That's why you practise, isn't it? So's you can get it right first time!"

George Watson laughed and ruffled Swot's hair. "You'd get on well with our Jimmy Charlton, Son. Your ideas are as daft as some of his! Come on. Let's be going. Ampton United are waiting for a whacking."

*     *     *

If Ampton United were in for a whacking, thought Swot just over an hour later, nobody had bothered to tell them. The match had been going for a couple of minutes and he couldn't remember a Rumney player having had a kick yet.

"Good, ain't they," said Kev as another quick interchange of passes put Ampton on the attack.

"Not bad, not bad," said Swot.

"We haven't had a kick yet."

"I know, I know."

"Unless you count Terry Potts kicking their left winger in the ankle."

"Give it time." Out on the pitch a well-positioned Norman Adlam intercepted an attempted through ball and laid it back to Corky Corcoran. "At least," said Swot, "our defence is looking stronger."

"We gotta win, though," said Kev, "and that means we've gotta score a goal."

Swot leaned into the UNCLE microphone.

"Control to manager," he snapped.

Outside, pacing the touchline so that he couldn't be overheard, was Brian Murrant. They saw his lips move, and "Manager here" crackled through the loudspeaker.

"Norman Adlam's playing too deep. Tell him he's got to get forward a bit more."

"Right." The loudspeaker nearly rose into the air as Brian yelled, "Norman! Get forward more!!"

Out on the pitch they saw the gangly midfield player stride over the halfway line. Seconds later he had the ball at his feet as Corky Corcoran's long kick was touched on to him.

The move threw Ampton into confusion. As Norman Adlam surged forward, the Ampton centre back didn't know whether to come to meet him or stay with George Watson who was on the edge of the penalty area and yelling for the ball.

"Push it through!" yelled Swot as the centre back finally made up his mind and moved towards Norman Adlam.

"Push it through!" bellowed Brain. Norman Adlam pushed it through.

George Watson controlled it with his left foot. He was on his own. The Ampton defence hadn't regrouped. It was a golden chance.

In fact it was so golden a chance that he tried to make absolutely certain. He switched the ball to his right foot. Then he tried to take it a bit nearer.

Given the little bit of time he needed, the Ampton goalkeeper charged off his line in a desperate attempt to smother the danger.

George Watson panicked. He had to shoot. He took a mighty swing at the ball and hit the ground with his toe.

Slowly, oh so slowly, the ball trickled along the ground and into the waiting arms of the grateful Ampton goalie.

"As I was saying," said Kev ruefully, "we gotta score."

Swot stared silently into space. It had been a great chance, and his dad had missed it!

But then again ... the move, *his* tactic ...

had worked neatly. If the other moves worked out as well, then they'd win. Just so long as they didn't give away a silly goal...

"Behind the ball!" he shouted as the Ampton goalkeeper, recovering quickly from the let-off George Watson had given him, took two steps and walloped the ball upfield. "Brian, get them back behind the ball!"

Out on the touchline they saw Brian Murrant yell through his cupped hands. It made no difference. What with the excitement of their attack and near miss, Rumney's defence had moved too far forward. They watched helplessly as the Ampton goalkeeper's kick sailed over their heads and the opposing team's tall striker set off in pursuit.

Seeing the danger, Corky Corcoran sprinted off his line. For one moment Swot thought he was going to win the race. But no. Lengthening his stride, the Ampton striker reached the ball a split second before the goalkeeper, pushed it past him and ran it gently into the Rumney net.

"I don't believe it," groaned Swot.

"I do," said Kev.

Swot buried his head in his hands. "One down."

"When we should have been one up," said Kev. "Fifteen minutes gone and it's the same old story."

Swot looked at his watch. Fifteen minutes gone. Only fifteen minutes. Plenty of time left. "Control to manager," he said into the microphone. "Act positive, Brian! Tell them to keep it going! The goal will come."

He smiled encouragingly at Kev. And crossed his fingers.

"Well, it ain't come yet, has it?" said Kev, as the teams trooped off at half-time. "That goal."

"Have we looked in trouble though?" asked Swot. "I ask you. Have we?"

"Not much," conceded Kev. "Only those times when your dad got the ball."

Swot ignored the jibe. "They've just got to keep it going," he said. "You watch. This is where the circuit training starts to pay off."

"It's going to have to," said Kev. "Look." He was pointing at the corner flag nearest to where Brian Murrant's car was parked. The flag had been hanging limply all throughout the first half. Now it was flapping wildly.

"Wind?" said Swot. "We haven't had any."

"Well, we have now," said Kev gloomily. "And it's against us."

And so Rumney kicked off for the second half with the wind against them.

"Get them to keep it on the deck," Swot had instructed Brian "Jimmy Charlton" Murrant during the interval. "That way Ampton's wind advantage won't count so much."

For a while, Rumney looked to have taken notice of what their new manager had said. A good move down the right between Baz Lucas and the Rumney right back Keith Burwood saw Lucas win a corner as an Ampton defender was forced to come across and stop him with a sliding tackle.

Swot spoke urgently into the UNCLE microphone. "Bring Norman Adlam up to use his height!" Brian Murrant echoed the instruction and Norman Adlam duly galloped up the pitch to station himself in the penalty area.

He wasted his energy. As Baz Lucas ran in to take the kick, George Watson came haring out towards him. "Short one!" he bellowed.

It was the worst thing that could have happened. Lucas was clearly caught in two minds. He didn't know whether to plant the ball into the goalmouth as he'd originally planned, or respond to the ear-splitting yell of George Watson.

Still confused, he took his eye off the ball. The effect was dramatic. Instead of hitting the ball cleanly into the goalmouth, he sliced the kick horribly. Up into the air sailed the ball, curving further and further away from the Ampton goal as the wind took it straight to the Ampton left winger.

"Oh, no! Get back!!"

Kev and Swot watched in horror as the

winger scampered away with the Rumney defenders stranded. It was like watching an action replay. The winger drew Keith Burwood towards him and then clipped the ball into the path of his centre forward. Moments later Corky Corcoran was picking the ball out of the net.

"Two-nil," announced Kev flatly. "Two ruddy-nil."

"Two attacks and two goals," breathed Swot. "It can't be true."

"It is," said Kev. "What are you gonna do about it, then, Mr Manager?"

The loudspeaker crackled. "What are we gonna do?" pleaded Brian.

Kev's patience was finally exhausted. "You can take his dad off for a start!" he yelled into the UNCLE microphone.

"Why?" asked Swot.

"Because he's useless, that's why!" yelled Kev.

Believe in yourself, thought Swot. All the best managers had unshakeable belief in themselves. "Control to manager," he announced. "Tell them to keep playing the way they are, Brian. They're playing well. The goals will come."

"The goals will come!" scoffed Kev. "And who's gonna bring them – Father Christmas?"

Out on the pitch the Rumney players were looking as disconsolate as Kev. Trudging back to the centre circle to kick off again, only one of them looked as though he still wanted to play.

"Come on, lads!" yelled George Watson, shaking his fist in the air. "We can do it! Come on!"

For a moment his enthusiasm worked. From the kick-off the ball was laid out to Baz Lucas. The wiry youngster took it forward. He beat one man, then another, before he was pulled down by a third Ampton defender.

Swot's heart leapt as the referee blew for a free kick. "Plan B4!" he screamed into the UNCLE microphone.

He held his breath as Brian Murrant relayed the message and Terry Potts moved forward to take the kick. The group of Rumney players huddled round the penalty spot in their Plan B4 positions. Just so long as they could remember where to run. Surely they would, after all that practice?

The answer was: no, not all of them. One player got it wrong.

It wasn't Terry Potts, who swung the free kick over into the perfect position.

It wasn't Baz Lucas, who made his decoy run towards the penalty spot at just the right time.

Neither was it Polo Pirelli, running towards the near post, nor Keith Burwood, running towards the far post.

And it wasn't Norman Adlam either. Just as plan B4 dictated he arrived late, all ready to score with a solid header.

No, it was George Watson who got it wrong.

Instead of making his decoy run in the direction of the corner flag he went for the ball and, in the process, clattered into Norman Adlam.

"Dad!" screamed Swot. "You idiot!" He buried his head in his hands.

And so it was that Simon "Swot" Watson missed the first goal Rumney scored under his managership. The first he knew of it was when Kev screamed in his ear. "Goal! Goal!! Wah-hooo!!!"

"What! How?!" he cried.

"Straight into the net!" yelled Kev. "Terry Potts' free kick went straight in! Yeah!!"

Unseen by Swot, the disaster of plan B4 had turned into an unexpected triumph. The sight of the Rumney players running everywhere, topped by that of George Watson and Norman Adlam slamming into each other and collapsing in a heap, had given the Ampton goalkeeper just too much to look at. Mesmerized, he'd taken his eye off the ball and allowed it to sail into the net.

"Come on!" urged Swot. "Come on!"

The loudspeaker crackled. "Your dad's injured," said Brian's voice.

George Watson, having disentangled himself from Norman Adlam, was limping heavily back to the centre circle for the kick-off.

"What bad luck," said Kev brightly. "You'll have to sub him."

"Who with?"

"Adie Mason," said Kev, pointing out of the car window towards the skinny, ginger-haired player who'd begun to warm up by sprinting along the touchline. "He's a forward."

"True."

"And Adie Mason's fast," added Kev. "Your dad's only going at half speed, and for him that is S-L-O-W."

Swot nodded. Much as he hated to admit it, Kev was right. His dad was limping badly. "Control to manager," he said into the microphone. "Tell him to come off, Brian."

"George!" they heard Brian Murrant yell. "Come off!"

Swot didn't have to hear his dad's reply. The look on his face and the way he shook his fist told him it hadn't been polite.

Brian Murrant confirmed this a moment

later. "He won't come off," crackled the loudspeaker.

"He's gotta come off," cried Kev. "Tell him he's gotta come off!"

Swot glared at Kev. He was going to make the decisions, and as far as he was concerned Kev was just a bit too enthusiastic to get his dad off the pitch. "Leave him on, Brian," he snapped.

"What?" said a disbelieving Kev.

"Put Baz Lucas into the middle," continued Swot, "push Terry Potts forward a bit and move my dad out to the wing."

"You sure?" crackled Brian.

Swot gave Kev a determined stare. "I'm sure."

Kev shrugged. He wouldn't change Swot's mind, he could tell that. "Yeah, Brian. He's sure."

There might have been something sprained about George Watson's ankle but his tonsils were still in fine working order. "Come on, lads!" they could hear him bawling as he hobbled up and down the wing. "Come on! We're getting on top."

What was more, Swot could see that he was right. They *were* getting on top. Terry Potts' fluke goal had given Rumney a new lease of life, that was obvious. But more than that, and in a way that Swot couldn't quite put his finger on, the team seemed to be playing together more.

An Ampton attack was broken up by Keith Burwood, who quickly switched the ball inside to Terry Potts. Rumney's captain looked up and saw that Baz Lucas had found some space on the right of the Ampton penalty box. He hit a low pass straight to him.

"Baz!" screamed George Watson from the far wing. He began to hobble inside. "My ball, Baz!" An Ampton defender moved towards him. "Baz!" yelled George Watson again as loudly as he could. Another Ampton defender moved his way.

Baz Lucas looked up. A gap had opened in the Ampton defence. He had a clear run for goal. Quickly he dribbled forward into the Ampton penalty area. By the time the Ampton defenders realized that he wasn't going to pass to the yelling George Watson it was too late.

Baz Lucas had time to pick his spot and crack the ball into the net.

Rumney were level!

Swot was ecstatic. They were clearly on top now. Six minutes to go. One final push would do it. And who better than Sgt. Terry Potts to do the pushing!

"Control to manager," snapped Swot. "Terry Potts into midfield. Norman Adlam to the back four."

It was a brilliant move. Almost immediately an Ampton forward lost the ball to a crushing Terry Potts tackle. Getting the ball under control, the Rumney skipper began a surging run forward. Past one man he went, then another.

"Come on, Terry," urged Swot.

"Just like the Barfield game," said Kev as Terry Potts charged towards the Ampton penalty area, "when your dad got himself offside."

"So long as he doesn't do it again. . ."

"He won't," said Kev. "He can't. Look."

George Watson was clearly trying his hardest to get into the attack but his injury was stopping him. At one point he tried hopping, but it was no good. Terry Potts just swept past him, took two more steps forward and let fly.

Wallop!

The ball hit the back of the Ampton net like a cannonball.

"Yeahhh!!!" screamed Swot and Kev together.

Rumney 3 Ampton 2!

There was no way back for Ampton. A couple of half-hearted attacks were easily snuffed out by the cock-a-hoop Rumney defence and then the final whistle went.

"Genius," yelled Kev, grabbing Swot by the hand. "Sheer genius!"

Swot tried to look cool, but his insides were leaping for joy. "Control to manager," he said into the UNCLE microphone. "Closing down transmissions."

"Hallelujah," said Brian Murrant. "Over and out."

"Over," said Swot. "But not out. Not yet. Rumney are on the march!"

# CHAPTER 11

## Blue Ankles and Cold Feet

One person who wasn't on the march was George Watson. In fact, it was as much as he could do to walk.

"How's the ankle, Dad?" said Swot after they'd enjoyed a celebration tea of fish and chips.

"Not so good, Son." George Watson pulled down the corner of his right sock to reveal an ankle with a decidedly blue tinge to it.

"Nasty bruise," said Swot sternly. "That needs an ice pack on it. Straight away," he added as his dad winced with pain.

"All right, don't nag," said George Watson. "Crikey, anyone'd think you were the Rumney manager." He hobbled across to the refrigerator and removed the ice tray from the freezer compartment. Tipping the ice cubes into a small polythene bag he hopped back to the table and sat down. He pressed the bag against his ankle. "Aaagggh!"

"Cold?"

"What do you think?" moaned George Watson.

"Maybe you should have come off when

I. . ." He bit his tongue quickly. "What I mean is . . . er . . . when I saw Jimmy Charlton call you."

"Come off!" exploded George Watson. "Me? Not likely!" He stuck his chin out in a determined fashion. "Couldn't he see we were getting on top? If I'd come off it would have destroyed our rhythm. Now, if I'd been the manager. . ."

It was the chance Swot had been waiting for. Ever since he'd seen his dad coming out of Jack Pettigrew's house on the night of the interview he'd been wanting to find out why he wanted the job. Not being able to say anything for fear of giving the game away had been almost too much to bear.

"You wouldn't want to be manager, would you?" he asked nonchalantly.

George Watson looked at him. "Why not? Don't you think I could do it?"

"Well . . . no . . . of course you could. It's just that . . . well . . . you're a player. You've always been a player."

"Not for much longer, Son."

Swot couldn't believe his ears. "Why not?"

"Well, I mean, I'm not getting any younger, am I? No, I reckon it's nearly time I was hanging up the old boots. In fact. . ."

"What?"

"I was thinking of making this my last season. It'd have been definite if this Jimmy Charlton hadn't turned up out of the blue and beat me to the manager's job. I went after it, y'know."

"You did?" said Swot innocently.

George Watson nodded. "Aye. Had an interview round at Jack Pettigrew's place. But he went for Jimmy Smart-Alec instead. And after today's game I can see why. He's a shrewd cookie, all right." He applied the ice pack and winced again. "But let's hope he's not too smart, eh Son?"

"Not too smart?" said Swot. "Why?"

George Watson winked. "Because this ankle feels like it's had a ton of spuds tipped on it, that's why. I'll be lucky if it's better in time for the game against Hamwell on Tuesday night. And if Jimmy Charlton's smart enough to spot I'm not fit then he'll be tempted to leave me out."

"But if you're not fit, he should leave you out, shouldn't he?"

"Course he should. But I'm going to play in that game, ankle or no ankle."

He rested his foot gingerly on the chair opposite. Swot thought he could see it turning bluer by the minute. "Can you keep a secret, Son?" he said.

Swot gulped. "Yes," he said. Underneath the kitchen table he crossed his fingers.

"I haven't told anyone this," said George Watson. "But I've been doing some counting up. And I reckon Tuesday's game will be number 499 for me in a Rumney shirt. Just think of that. Not bad, eh?"

"So the last game of the season will be number 500," said Swot.

"A good way to go out, eh, Son? Specially if we stay up."

Swot nodded. "We will," he said.

"That's my boy. Number one supporter. And remember," said George Watson, pointing to an ankle that was now nearly as blue as an Everton supporter's scarf, "no telling. I'm playing on Tuesday if it's the last thing I do!"

"Bad news," hissed Kev.

Swot peered into the telephone as if he was looking for his friend at the other end of the line. "How do you know?"

"He just told me, that's how!"

Swot blinked. Why did conversations with Kev always go this way? He thought backwards. They'd been sitting at the kitchen table a minute ago, discussing his dad's ankle. The telephone had rung. His dad had hopped out into the hallway to answer it, muttering something about giving his ankle a fitness test as he went. Moments later he'd hopped back again to tell Swot it was for him. He couldn't have had time to tell Kev about it.

Swot tried again. "It's bad all right. It's gone all blue."

Kev sounded irritated. "What has?"

"My dad's ankle, of course."

"What the heck has your dad's ankle got to do with it?"

"Bad news," said Swot. "You said he'd just told you!"

"He didn't say anything about his ankle," said Kev. "And what's bad news about that anyway?"

"Well, nothing I suppose. He still wants to play Tuesday night."

"Now that *is* bad news," said Kev.

"All right," said Swot icily, "so if my dad's ankle isn't bad news, then what is? Who *have* you been talking to?"

"Our Brian. And it's bad news."

"What is?"

"He wants out. Finito. No more Jimmy Charlton."

"But why?" hissed Swot. "Just when everything's working brilliantly."

"Dunno," said Kev. "But I reckon the bobby in the panda car might've had something to do with it."

"Bobby? What bobby? When?"

"After the game. You'd just gone when that bobby ... y'know, the one with the flat head who gives Terry Potts a lift..."

Swot would have described PC Roland Cape as having a flat cap rather than a flat head, but he let it pass. "Yes, I know the one," he said.

"Well, he comes up to Brian and says, 'Excuse me, sir, I'd like you to help me with my enquiries'."

"Why? What sort of enquiries?"

"Nothing. He just wanted to know where Terry Potts was. But it put the wind up our Brian for some reason. He was shaking like a jelly on the way home. Nearly drove us round the bend a couple of times, he did."

"And you think that's why he wants out?"

"That. And the other thing."

"What other thing?"

"Money. He reckons he don't need the money now. Old man Pettigrew was so chuffed about the win he gave him a hundred pounds instead of the fifty they'd agreed. Add that to what he reckons he'll get from tomorrow's car boot sale and he's got enough for another telly."

Swot had worked it out already. "You don't mean…"

"Yep. That's the bad news. I'll have no hold over him. He says Monday night he'll ring Jack Pettigrew and spill the beans."

"He can't!"

"Oh, yes he can," said Kev down the line. "Unless we can come up with some way of … y'know…"

"Stopping him."

"Right," said Kev. "And quick."

Swot's mind switched into gear. Tactics. It just had to be a matter of tactics. Think it through.

What was the key factor? Brian would have enough money after the car boot sale. So, question: what would stop Brian getting enough money? Answer: sabotaging tomorrow's car boot sale!

"Will you be at this sale tomorrow?"

"Course I will," said Kev. "This could be the last ten per cent."

"Right," said Swot. An idea was forming.
"And you'll be in Brian's car?"

"Natch," said Kev.

"OK. I'll see you there. And somehow ... I
don't care how you do it, Kev ... but somehow, bring the UNCLE gear with you."

# CHAPTER 12

## Brian Gets the Boot

St Winifred's Church was old and grey, but had a brand new car park alongside it. Between the two was a low stone wall. On the churchyard side, this wall was lined with thick and ancient shrubbery. On the car park side of the wall, close by the entrance, a long table had been set up. Behind this table sat two men.

Two very large men.

Swot handed over his 20p entrance money to the smaller of the two large men, a man who was merely barn-door sized. "Money paid," growled Barn Door.

Hearing this, the larger of the two large

men, a man who would have made a haystack feel inferior, stood aside. "Enter," announced Haystack.

Swot entered, shivering as he passed through Haystack's shadow and out the other side. He looked around. More cars, loaded to their roof racks with anything that might sell, were arriving by the minute.

Haystack and Barn Door were treating the cars in an even more menacing fashion than the pedestrians. As each arrived, Haystack would stand in front of it, hands on hips. Barn Door would open the driver's door and shove one of his giant hands inside. Only when it emerged clutching the entrance fee did Haystack move aside and let the car through.

As Swot watched them, his idea, vague last night, was now starting to take shape. Just as long as Kev had done his bit...

"OK, what's the plan?" Like a magician's assistant arriving on cue, Kev had popped out of the milling crowd of bargain-hunters to appear in front of him.

"Quick," said Swot. "I want you to go over

there, behind the bushes, with the UNCLE system. OK?"

"Ah. . ." said Kev. His face clouded over.

"You *have* got it?" said Swot.

"Sure I have. Sort of."

"What does that mean?"

"It means I've got it. But it's sort of . . . not easy to get at."

"What are you on about? Where is it?"

"Over there."

Kev was pointing across to where the sellers' cars were grouped in a circle like wagons preparing to be stormed by Indians on the warpath.

Swot looked in the direction of his finger. First he spotted, on the far side of the circle, Brian Murrant's rusty old car. Then he saw Brian himself, busily unloading this and that from the car's boot.

"You haven't left it in the car? He'll find it!"

"Course I haven't! You think I'm stupid? It's well out of sight. That's why it's not easy to get at."

Swot had a sinking feeling. "Where is it, Kev?" he said, quietly.

"Under Brian's car."

"Under!"

"Yeah, under! Where the spare tyre lives." He gave Swot a belligerent look. "What was I s'posed to do with it, eh? Stick it down me trouser-leg? You try hiding a great big holdall so's your brother don't know you've got it."

Swot held up his hands. "OK, OK. So how do you reckon we get it out? Dig a tunnel?"

"Ah!" said Kev brightly. "Now, I've been thinking about that."

"Ye-es?"

"Well ... I thought ... well, I thought one of us could ... like ... sort of attract his attention while the other one sort of ... sort of crawled underneath and got it out."

"And who's doing the crawling?" asked Swot.

"You?"

"You," said Swot. "And when you get UNCLE out, this is what you're going to do..."

Swot made his way across the church car park to where Brian Murrant had set up shop. The nearer he got, the more serious he realized the situation was. Brian had managed to gather together a whole stack of stuff from somewhere. If he managed to sell even half of it he'd have enough money to buy his replacement telly and retire from football management.

This plan just had to work.

"Howdo, Brian," he said.

Brian Murrant looked up from the boot of his car. "What do you want?" he said.

"Nothing, nothing," said Swot. "Got some interesting stuff here, haven't you?" He bent down and picked up a large vase from amongst the wares that Brian had laid out on an old blanket.

"Watch it, watch it!" said Brian Murrant, hurrying round the side of the car and plucking the vase from Swot's hands. "I want to sell that."

"Just looking," said Swot. It was a good start. He'd got Brian away from the car. Now it was up to Kev.

"Our Kevin's got you to come down here, has he?" said Brian. "Told you that's it after this morning, has he? Bye-bye Rumney."

"He did mention it," said Swot.

"Typical," said Brian. "Going behind my back."

You never spoke a truer word, thought Swot, as out of the corner of his eye he saw Kev nip between two startled shoppers, throw himself to the ground, and then proceed to crawl on his stomach towards Brian's car.

Brian was looking determined. "Well, don't think you can get round me. You can't."

Swot shrugged. "Ah well," he said. "I thought I might, but I can see you've made up your mind." Kev had crawled round to the side of the car. "Pity. But there we are."

Brian Murrant looked at him doubtfully. "You're taking it very well."

"Accept the inevitable, that's my motto," said Swot.

146

"Good," said Brian. "So that's all right, then. Now, if you'll excuse me I've got more unloading to do."

"Wait!" cried Swot. Kev was underneath the car, tugging desperately at the UNCLE holdall. If Brian turned round now the game would be up. He had no choice but to put the next part of his plan into action and hope for the best.

"What now?" said Brian.

"Well ... er ... No, it probably wasn't you they were talking about."

"What wasn't me? Who?"

"Them." Swot jerked a thumb in the direction of Haystack and Barn Door at the entrance. "When I came in just now they were saying something about overcharging somebody. Car registration..." He glanced quickly at the number plate on Brian's car. "KTR something."

"997Y?" asked Brian, reeling off the rest of his car's number.

"Might have been. How much did you pay to come in?"

"Car fee? Five pounds."

"Ah," said Swot. "Could have been you, then. It should have only been two today. Special offer."

"Two? Not five?"

"Right," said Swot. "Right!"

Behind Brian's back Kev had emerged triumphant with the UNCLE holdall in his arms. "You want to go over and check, Brian," Swot said loudly. "I mean, three pound's three pounds. It's a bit more in the kitty if you get a refund, eh?"

"Right," agreed Brian Murrant. Moments later he was on his way towards the entrance.

"Quick," hissed Swot as Kev dashed up to him, handed over the UNCLE hearing-aid unit, and then dashed off again through the crowded car park. "And whatever you do, don't let him see you!"

Swot's head switched from side to side like a spectator at Wimbledon, looking one way at Brian Murrant as he pushed through to the giant gate-men, and then the other at Kev as he dived over the churchyard wall and ducked along towards their money table before disappearing into the bushes.

A sharp click from the hearing aid told him that Kev had turned the UNCLE control unit on. And then, very faintly, he heard Brian Murrant's voice.

"KTR 997Y," he was saying. "You charged me too much to get in."

"Too much?" Swot heard Barn Door say. "I did not charge you too much."

"You did," said Brian.

Swot saw Haystack get to his feet. Moments later his voice was ringing in Swot's ears. "I do hope you're not going to argue, mate."

"N-no," stammered Brian. "No." He turned away.

Watching from the other side of the car park, Swot timed his moment perfectly. He put the hearing-aid unit to his lips. "Not with you, anyway, you great big dollop!"

Over by the entrance, the effect was immediate. Haystack moved menacingly towards Brian Murrant as out of the UNCLE loudspeaker that Kev had turned on came loud and clear, "Not with you, anyway, you great big dollop!"

"Oy," said Haystack, "who are you calling a dollop?"

"What?" said Brian Murrant turning round.

"Great big dollop," said Haystack. "I said who are you calling a great big dollop?"

"Nobody," said Brian Murrant. "I didn't."

Swot saw Brian turn away again. He put the hearing-aid unit to his lips once more. "It was your mate I was calling a great big dollop," he said. "You're a steaming great prune!"

"What!" yelled Barn Door as the insult rang out from the UNCLE loudspeaker. "A great big dollop, am I?"

"Eh?" It was Brian, sounding anxious.

"And I'm a steaming great prune, am I?" roared Haystack.

"I didn't say that!" Swot heard Brian Murrant cry. "I didn't say anything! I ... aaaggh!" Brian didn't finish what he was saying.

From his position, Swot could see why. Barn Door had taken his right arm, Haystack his left, and between them they'd hoisted Brian Murrant off the ground.

"I've just about had enough of this one," Barn Door was yelling as they carried a kicking Brian across the car park. "Haven't you, Jeremy?"

"I have, Gordon," Haystack agreed. "I certainly have."

"But I didn't..." squawked Brian.

"And you're not going to, mate," said Haystack.

"Not here. Not today. Not no-how," continued Barn Door.

As they reached Brian Murrant's car they let him go in unison. He landed with a nasty thud on the ground in front of Swot.

"Go on! Sling your hook!" growled Barn Door.

"Clear off," added Haystack. "Now."

"But..." pleaded Brian, "I haven't sold anything. I need the money. I..."

"Too bad."

"Shove off."

"Can I have my entrance money back then?"

"Gerroutofit!" yelled Barn Door and Haystack together.

Brian was beaten. He was worse off now than when he'd arrived. Not only had he not made any money, he'd lost his entrance money into the bargain.

As a dejected Brian, watched over by a glowering Haystack and a nasty-looking Barn Door, started to reload his car boot, Swot nipped quickly over to where Kev was packing the UNCLE gear away.

"Here," said Kev, handing Swot the holdall, "you'd better take this lot home."

"Good idea," said Swot. "I'll bring it round later. If Brian saw you with it and put two-and-two together..."

Kev made an exploding noise. "He'd go bananas. He'd go right up in the air..."

"Again," said Swot with a smile.

"Yeah!" hooted Kev. The tears started running down his face. "When those two gorillas carried our Brian away like a sack of coal ... I thought I was gonna die!"

Swot nodded happily. "And he's lost his entrance money."

"He has? Great! He'll definitely be a bit short of cash then, won't he?"

"Sad, eh?" said Swot. "No money."

"No time to get any before Tuesday night's game against Hamwell."

"No money, no replacement telly."

"No replacement telly, no giving up as Jimmy Charlton," crowed Kev. "Poor Brian."

"Poor Brian," echoed Swot.

"Aaaah," they said together.

# CHAPTER 13

## Come In, Number 9

"Appearance 499," said George Watson as he swung the van into its usual position alongside the Rumney pitch. "Who'd have believed it, eh?"

"Not me," said Swot. "You don't look old enough."

"I'm starting to feel it, Son." Carefully, George Watson put his foot on the ground.

"How's the ankle?" asked Swot.

"Fine, fine."

"Not hurting, then?"

George Watson gave him a look. "Who are you, the manager or summat? It's fine. I just don't want to put it under unnecessary strain before the game, that's all."

"You *are* fit, then?"

"As a fiddle, Son. You watch me go! We're on for another win today, I can feel it in my bones." He winked and patted his dodgy ankle. "Specially this one."

Swot waited until his dad disappeared into the Rumney changing room and then dived across to join Kev in the front seats of Brian Murrant's car.

"Your dad recovered, has he?" asked Kev at once.

"Er ... yes," said Swot, hesitantly.

"Gave him a late fitness test, did you?" asked Kev, suspiciously. "Get him kicking a few Brussels sprouts round the shop?"

"He's fine, I tell you. Never felt fitter."

"Oh," said Kev. "He's playing, then?"

"Course," said Swot. "Same team again. Never change a winning combination, you know that."

"Till they lose," said Kev. "Then it'll be too late."

"Rumney are not going to lose," said Swot

firmly. "All we've got to do is play the way we ended against Ampton and we're home and dry. Now, is Brian wired up?"

"Yep," said Kev. He pointed over to the figure sitting alone in the Rumney dug-out. "Ready to go."

"Happy about life, is he?" chuckled Swot, flicking the UNCLE microphone to ON.

"No, I'm ruddy well not," growled Brian through the loudspeaker.

"Never mind," said Swot. "One more game after tonight and then it'll be all over. Rumney will have been saved from relegation, you'll have your new telly and the world will be a happier place all round."

"Yeah, yeah," growled Brian Murrant, clearly in no mood to think about happier worlds. "Come on, then, what's the team? I gotta be going in there soon."

In the car Swot checked his list. "Same as Saturday. But leave Terry Potts in midfield and Norman Adlam at the back. The way we finished."

"That mean your dad's on the wing as well?" asked Brian.

Swot hesitated. He'd been thinking about that. Had it been his imagination, or had things really gone better against Ampton after his dad had limped out to the wing?

It was his imagination. "Striker," he snapped. "As per usual."

"As per usual," muttered Kev. "That's what I was afraid of."

Away in the distance the Rumney village clock struck seven.

As if he'd been waiting for the signal, the referee blew his whistle. Rumney kicked off. Their second match under the management of Jimmy Charlton, alias Brian Murrant, alias Simon "Swot" Watson, was under way.

Rumney started brightly.

A quick burst by Baz Lucas saw him outstrip the Hamwell right back and cut inside. He looked up.

"Baz!" yelled George Watson from the edge of the penalty area.

Lucas stopped. He switched the ball to his right foot and, as the Hamwell sweeper came across to challenge, rolled it gently back to George Watson.

Wallop!

The Hamwell goalkeeper jumped up and touched the crossbar with his fingertips to show that he'd have had the shot covered if it had been on target. It hadn't. The Rumney groundsman was already on his way to find his ladder.

"Forgot to get his head over the ball," said Swot.

"Yeah," muttered Kev, "and got the ball over everyone else's head instead."

"Still," said Swot, "it looks like his ankle's OK."

"Great," said Kev without enthusiasm.

Hamwell bounced back quickly. A short goal kick sent their right back surging through the middle. Baz Lucas, still wondering how

George Watson could get a ball so high off the ground without the aid of a rocket launcher, had given him too much of a start and was in no position to tackle back.

Seeing the danger, Sergeant Terry Potts came sailing across from midfield and tackled the Hamwell player as though he was a bank robber on the run. Pheep! The referee blew his whistle and marched across to the scene of the crime.

"Yellow card!" said Kev. "And we've only been playing five minutes! Who is that right back?"

"Whybrow," answered Swot. "The Hamwell captain. He could give us a lot of trouble."

He wasn't wrong. Ten minutes later the same player pushed forward again. He dribbled up to Terry Potts. A quick shimmy, and then he was going one way as Terry Potts went the other.

The police sergeant turned and gave chase. Whybrow heard him coming. He slowed slightly to let Potts get nearer. Glancing up he saw that the referee was unsighted. Then, just as Terry Potts reached him, Whybrow threw himself to the ground with a cry of agony.

"Aaaagggghhh!"

Pheeep!

"Ref?" appealed Terry Potts as the man in black ran over. "I never touched him. Honest!"

As the referee finger-wagged and pointed to his breast pocket, Swot thought quickly. It was obvious what the referee was saying. Another incident like that, and Sgt. T. Potts would be taking an early bath.

"Control to manager," barked Swot.

"What?" answered Brian. Clearly he wasn't happy.

"Switch Potts to back four. Norman Adlam to midfield."

"What!" yelled Kev. "Are you bonkers! Terry Potts *is* the midfield! Putting him in the back four is like trying to win a war with Rambo in the kitchen peeling spuds."

"He'll be no good at all to us if he gets sent off, will he?" argued Swot. "That full back is too quick for him."

"And Normie Adlam, the walking tent-pole, is gonna do better, is he?" Kev shook his head. "Not a chance."

The game carried on. A promising Rumney attack saw Baz Lucas win a corner which came to nothing when George Watson hared out to the flag and called for a short one, then, in his excitement, kicked the return pass into touch. "Sorry, lads!" he yelled, as he ran back.

From the throw-in, Whybrow, the Hamwell right back, made another surging run forward. This time, instead of meeting the rugged Terry Potts, he came up against the tall figure of Norman Adlam. Whybrow feinted to go one way, then darted the other. Adlam hardly moved. He simply stuck out one of his long legs and poked the ball off Whybrow's toe and straight to an unmarked Keith Burwood.

The surprise loss of the ball caught Hamwell off balance. Burwood found Baz Lucas out on the left.

Lucas cut inside. Once again George Watson was on the edge of the area, yelling for the ball.

"Don't give it to him," urged Kev.

For once Swot agreed. "Normie Adlam's free!" he yelled.

After winning the ball, the gangly midfield man had carried on moving forward. Now, as he ran into the penalty box, Baz Lucas spotted him.

He stopped, steadied himself, and then crossed the ball.

"Oh, rubbish cross," groaned Swot.

Lucas had mis-kicked, with the result that his intended chip had turned into a cross which, instead of floating gently into the centre, was now whistling across the face of the goal a metre off the ground.

"Who's gonna reach that?" cried Kev.

"Norman Adlam!" yelled Swot, unable to believe his eyes.

"Goal!!!" screamed Kev.

"Yeahh!!!!"

The ball was in the net!

Norman Adlam had flung himself full length – and his length was fuller than any-body's – at the ball as it came across and scored with a diving header.

One up to Rumney!

"OK, OK," said Kev as the teams went in for half-time with Rumney still ahead. "You were right. Again. Normie Adlam's playing a blinder. That right back can't get past him."

Over the loudspeaker they could hear Brian Murrant giving Swot's half-time pep-talk. "Keep going," he was saying dully. "You're doing all right. If we win one-nil it's as good as ten-nil. Don't give them a chance to break."

"He sounds like he's reading the news at a funeral," said Swot.

"Being blackmailed does that to you, I suppose," said Kev.

"Defend in depth," droned Brian. "All back behind the ball."

"Boss! You sure, Boss?"

"Your dad," said Kev, as if Swot wouldn't be able to recognize the voice immediately.

"I mean," said George Watson, his excitement fairly crackling out of the UNCLE loudspeaker, "they say attack's the best form of defence, don't they? We've had 'em pinned in their own half since we scored. I say we should go for 'em! Get the second! Finish 'em off!"

Swot spoke sharply into the UNCLE microphone. "Control to manager. Defend in depth. Repeat, defend in depth."

"My instructions," echoed Brian Murrant, with great honesty, "are defend in depth."

"OK," said George Watson. "Anything you say, Boss."

"Your dad didn't sound like he approved," said Kev as the teams came on to the field.

"No," said Swot. He was starting to think the unthinkable: that maybe Rumney *could* manage without Watson Snr.

That view was reinforced almost immediately.

Hamwell kicked off. The ball was played back to their midfield and from there walloped forward towards the Rumney penalty area.

By then, George Watson had already taken his manager's instructions to heart and started defending in depth. Having managed to get himself from the centre-circle to the Rumney back four in five seconds flat, he leapt up to try to head the ball away. Unfortunately he'd really needed six seconds. He hadn't got back quite far enough. As the ball bounced off his head it went, not away from the Rumney goal, but towards it.

"Oh, no!" moaned Swot as the ball sailed over the head of Corky Corcoran as he stood on his own penalty spot. The whole Rumney defence turned and watched as George Watson's accidental back-header started to come down towards the empty Rumney net . . . and bounced off the top of the crossbar for a corner.

"Phew!" said Kev. "I dunno about you, but my nerves ain't gonna last out for the rest of this game."

"Mine neither," said Swot. "Unless I do something about it. Control to manager.

Control to manager. George Watson to the wing."

"Eh?" said the loudspeaker. "You sure?"

"Repeat. George Watson to left wing."

Kev raised an eyebrow. "Think he'll take any notice?"

"He'd better," said Swot grimly.


Out on the pitch, George Watson took notice – for a while.

He ran up and down the wing. He called for the ball. He yelled at people to get stuck in. He called for the ball. He bellowed at people to keep going, play it simple, defend in depth. And he called for the ball, which never came.

For twenty minutes, as Rumney soaked up the pressure Hamwell were putting on them, George Watson patrolled the left wing like a lion on a long leash. Twenty minutes, in which time he didn't touch the ball and Rumney didn't have a moment's anxiety.

Whybrow, the speedy Hamwell right back, broke out of defence again. Frustrated at continually having his surges through mid-field closed down by the lanky legs of Norman Adlam, he'd decided to try his luck out on the touchline. George Watson saw him coming, and moved in to challenge. So did Norman Adlam, who'd been having his most enjoyable game of the season.

The collision was spectacular.

Norman Adlam tackled Whybrow, George Watson tackled Norman Adlam, and Whybrow tackled George Watson. The three of them fell in a heap, leaving the ball to run gently into touch.

"Looks like your dad's ankle's gone," said Kev.

Swot had to agree. George Watson had been the last of the three players to get up and he was hobbling badly, his hand down at his ankle.

"Control to manager," said Swot decisively. "Bring on the sub."

"Who for?" said Brian Murrant.

Swot paused. He looked out at his dad, now down on one knee. "George Watson."

"You sure?"

Swot was sure. It had to be done. "George Watson," he repeated. "My dad."

From the dug-out two boards appeared, one with the number 12 on it, the other the number 9. Moments later, substitute Adie Mason was running on to the pitch. "Slowly, George Watson walked off the pitch," commentated Kev.

"Walked?" said Swot. "Hobbled, you mean."

"No, walked. Look."

As he left the pitch George Watson was looking miserable, but walking normally. The only thing obviously not right about him was that in his hand he was carrying a football boot.

"His boot had come off," laughed Kev.

Swot's mouth fell open. "He wasn't injured at all!"

"And you've..."

"...just substituted him!" groaned Swot.

"Ah well. Right decision, wrong reason," said Kev.

Swot's mind was still in a turmoil as the game restarted with a free kick to Hamwell. Whybrow took it himself, floating a long ball into the Rumney goalmouth.

It presented little problem. Terry Potts, no longer having to cope with George Watson rushing back to help out, headed the ball away without difficulty. Norman Adlam, moving quickly out of defence, beat a Hamwell player to the clearance and played it quickly out to Adie Mason. The substitute set off down the wing like a greyhound.

"Fast, ain't he?" said Kev.

"Give it to Baz Lucas!" pleaded Swot.

Adie Mason did just that. Baz Lucas picked the ball up and held off a challenge as Mason cut inside. Then, as the substitute came level with him, Lucas slipped the ball into his path.

"He's lost it," said Kev as Adie Mason seemed to hit the ball too far ahead of himself.

"What do you expect?" said Swot. He was still feeling guilty. "He can't control the ball if he's going like a runaway train."

"Yep, the Hamwell number 4's got it," commentated Kev. "Adie's breathing down his neck though. He's catching him. He's ... goal!!! It's a goal!!"

"Yeah!!" Swot punched the air with delight and hurt his hand on the roof of the car.

Pressured by the knowledge that rocket Mason was behind him, the Hamwell number 4 had panicked. Instead of playing his back-pass safely he'd sent it spinning beyond the Hamwell goalkeeper and into his own net!

"An inspired substitution!" yelled Kev. "Can this boy do no wrong?"

"Seems not," said Swot. His guilty feelings about substituting his own dad suddenly faded. He felt his back straighten. A manager had to manage. Difficult decisions had to be made. There was no room for sentiment. Football could be a cruel game.

He grabbed the UNCLE microphone. "Control to manager!"

"Yeah," crackled Brian Murrant through the loudspeaker. Even a two-goal lead didn't seem to have cheered him up.

"Tell them to give Mason the ball every chance they get! Attack! Attack!"

And attack Rumney did. With Adie Mason haring up and down the wing – going nowhere most of the time, but getting there very quickly – Whybrow was fully occupied. With him tied up, Hamwell couldn't mount a single attack.

In the car, the excitement boiled over as the final whistle went.

"Control to manager," yelled Swot. "Tell them no training on Tuesday!"

"Yeah," yelled Kev into the microphone, "tell 'em to save themselves for next Saturday."

Swot was ecstatic. "The last game of the season! And we're gonna win it!"

"We're gonna win it!" echoed Kev.

"Rumney are going to stay up!" yelled Swot into UNCLE's microphone. "We're going to escape! What do you say to that, Brian?"

"Escape? Oh, no. Not if I have anything to do with it."

Swot was confused. He looked at the UNCLE loudspeaker. For the first time in its history it hadn't crackled. But, more than that, he couldn't understand why Brian sounded so gloomy.

"What do you mean? Come on, Brian, one more win and we're out of trouble! It'll all be over."

"I think it's all over right now," said the gloomy one.

More confusion. For some unaccountable reason, Kev was tugging at his sleeve. "Swot..."

Swot ignored him. "Control to manager," he shouted excitedly into the UNCLE microphone. "What're you going on about, Brian? Things are looking good!"

"Swot..." Kev tugged again.

"They're looking great!"

"No, they're not," said Kev.

"Eh?"

"They ain't looking at all. They've found us."

Swot looked at Kev. Kev poked a thumb

over his shoulder. Swot looked at where Kev's thumb was pointing.

Then he realized why the gloomy voice hadn't sounded like Brian Murrant. It hadn't been the voice of Brian Murrant.

He also realized why it had been coming through so loud and clear. It was because it hadn't had far to travel. Just from the car's open rear door.

"I think," said PC Roland Cape, with the serious look he practised in the mirror every morning, "you two have got some explaining to do. I've been getting some very funny programmes on my radio lately."

# CHAPTER 14

## A Bit of a Trial

To Swot it seemed more like a court room than the Rumney Town dressing room. Standing in the centre of the muddy floor, with Kev on his right and Brian Murrant on his left, it felt as if they were prisoners in the dock.

At one end of the Rumney dressing room, looking for all the world like three magistrates, sat:

- Terry Potts, police sergeant and Rumney skipper.
- Jack Pettigrew, wealthy butcher and Rumney Chairman.
- George Watson, greengrocer, Rumney's

longest-serving player and father of one of the accused.

Strung out on the benches lining the two sides of the changing-room walls sat the rest of the Rumney team – the jury.

"Hrmpph." Swot looked up as the tall figure in blue standing next to the treatment table cleared his throat. The picture was complete. PC Roland Cape was about to give evidence.

"Whilst proceeding in an easterly direction along Allotment Road in the direction of the Rumney Town Football Ground en route to the picking up of yourself, Sergeant Potts, I experienced a high whistling sound through my patrol car's communications system..."

"His what?" asked Jack Pettigrew.

"Radio," said Terry Potts.

"This whistling sound was shortly followed, as I drew nearer to the ground, by a voice. The voice said..." At this, PC Cape thumbed his notebook, " 'Control to manager. Tell them to give Mason the ball every chance they get! Attack! Attack!' "

"Mason? Perry Mason?"

"Adie Mason, I suspect, Mr Pettigrew."
PC Cape continued, "On turning into the
Rumney Town car park the voice became very
clear and excited. 'Tell them no training on
Tuesday,' it said. Consequently I suspected
that somewhere in the vicinity a person or
persons unknown were engaged in the illegal
transmitting of radio signals on police frequencies."

"Eh?" said Jack Pettigrew.

"He picked them up on his car radio," said
Terry Potts. "Carry on, Roly. And keep it
simple, there's a good lad."

"Vacating my car, I proceeded in a south-
erly direction towards an extremely rusty and
probably unroadworthy vehicle wherein I
discovered. . ."

"Roly. . ." warned Potts.

"I nicked these two," said PC Roland Cape,
"and this gear here." He pointed to the
Rumney treatment table, on which the
UNCLE equipment had been laid out.

"And I," yelled Jack Pettigrew, leaping to

his feet, "nicked t'manager!" He pointed angrily at Brian Murrant. "I want him charged, Sergeant Potts. Anything will do, so long as it's summat big. He made a reet fool of me."

"It wasn't my fault," cried Brian. "I had no choice. It was either that or..."

"OK, OK," said Terry Potts. He stood up himself now, as Jack Pettigrew sat down again.

If Potts looked big in his football gear, he looked positively massive in his sergeant's uniform. Swot felt two centimetres high as Potts addressed them in his sergeant's voice. "Right," he said, "let me recap."

If he'd had a pencil he would have licked it. Not having one, he had to make do with counting on his fingers. "One. Between the three of you, this here equipment – UNCLE or whatever it's called – was put together."

"Offences under the Wireless and Telegraphy Act," said Roland Cape, who'd been studying hard for his exams and welcomed the chance to show it.

"Two. You used it to convince Mr Petti-

grew here that one of you was a relative of Bobby Charlton..."

"False impersonation," said Roland Cape, "of an important ... er ... personage."

"Three. You then used this same equipment to send him instructions so as to make it appear he's a knowledgeable football manager..."

"Deception."

"Four," said Sergeant Potts, "this equipment broadcasts on police frequencies."

"Wireless and Telegraphy Act again. Frequency offence. For offending frequently."

"We didn't know about that one," said Kev. "Brian should have said."

"I wanted to! The first time I saw that panda car! But what good would it have done me, eh? You'd have split on me to the Wrinklies!"

PC Roland Cape made a sucking sound. "Blackmail," he said.

"And on top of all that," said Sergeant Terry Potts, "you..." looking at Swot, he held up his hand and waggled his thumb

"...you, young man, committed offence number five. You used this equipment so as to act as manager of Rumney Town Football Club from the back of a car!"

"Using a transport vehicle for a purpose for which it was not intended," intoned PC Roland Cape, "offence under Pirate Radio legislation..." He stopped, as Terry Potts held up a giant hand.

"Pretty serious charges, eh?"

"Yes, sir," said Swot, hoping that pleading guilty would count in his favour.

"Yeah, but..." began Kev boldly, then sank into an equally meek, "Yes, sir." Brian Murrant just nodded and kept his head down.

"Pretty serious," repeated Terry Potts. "And as a senior member of Her Majesty's Constabulary, honour bound to uphold the rule of law, I must tell you that I take a very dim view of what I've heard here today."

"Yes, sir," said Swot.

"As I expect your father does."

"Eh?" George Watson looked as though

he'd just snapped out of a trance. "Yes. Yes, you're right there, Flower. I mean, you're right there, Sergeant Potts."

"You've deceived all of us," Terry Potts went on, waving his uniformed arm with its three stripes round the dressing room. "Hasn't he, lads?"

"Yes, Sergeant Potts," chorused the Rumney players.

"You mean..." began Norman Adlam.

Corky Corcoran finished the statement for him. "We've had a kid for a manager for the past week? Right, that is what he means."

"Then," said Norman Adlam, as things started to sink in, "that training session last Tuesday. That was down to you, was it?" Swot nodded.

"Two hours of torture, that was!" cried Adlam. He looked as though the memory still hurt.

"I had to have a day off work after that," joined in Baz Lucas. "Me legs ached so much."

"And mine," echoed Keith Burwood. "I

couldn't get out of bed. I had to have a day off work an' all."

"You haven't got a job," said Norman Adlam.

"Yeah ... well..." said Burwood. "If I'd had one I'd have needed a day off from it after that training!"

"Circuit training, sprints, press–ups," groaned Corky Corcoran as the memories came flooding back. "And that free kick practising. A whole hour on that..."

"Shall I add grievous bodily harm to the list, Sarge?" asked PC Roland Cape helpfully.

"Possibly," said Terry Potts. "Possibly. Except for one thing."

"And what's that?" growled Jack Pettigrew.

"That training session did us a power of good."

The room fell silent. Then Baz Lucas spoke up. "He's right. So did the free kick practice. It paid off against Ampton, didn't it?"

The other players nodded in agreement.

"In fact," said Terry Potts, removing his sergeant's jacket and putting a Rumney scarf round his neck, "speaking as a Rumney player, I would say the whole episode has done the team a power of good."

"Right," nodded Baz Lucas. "The tactics have been magic. Look at the defence. They've never played better."

"And you've looked like scoring, Baz," said Corky Corcoran, "which is near enough miraculous."

"Putting me at the back today was a shrewd move," said Terry Potts. "I admit it, I'd have been in trouble if I'd stayed in midfield."

"What about my goal!" yelled Norman Adlam. "The switch round gave me a goal!"

"And me," joined in Adie Mason.

"Super-sub Mason," agreed Terry Potts, "and all down to the manager."

Swot smiled sheepishly. Brian was starting to look a bit relieved.

Kev stepped forward. It was time for an appeal from the lawyer for the defence. "Two wins!" he said boldly. "My man here has given Rumney Town two wins on the trot!"

He paused dramatically, allowing his appeal

to sink in. Then he spoke again. "One more win, against Lipton on Saturday, and Rumney will escape relegation! Think about that!"

He gazed around the dressing room. "I rest my holdall!" It didn't sound quite right, but never mind.

Terry Potts looked at Jack Pettigrew. "Well, Mr Chairman, what do you say? Do you still want to press charges?"

Jack Pettigrew thought for a moment. "Two wins on the trot," he nodded. He looked at Swot. "Can you mek it three, young man?"

"Definitely," said Swot.

"You sound reet confident. Lipton are second in't table, y'know. They'll be looking to beat us to win t'league."

"That means they'll be pressing forward, Mr Chairman. We can play a 1-4-4-1 formation with a sweeper and hit them on the break."

Jack Pettigrew's eyebrows lifted. He looked at Terry Potts. "Well . . . . there's nowt to lose – drop the charges!"

"What d'you reckon, lads?" said Terry Potts, gazing round the dressing room. "Swot here for manager to the end of the season?"

"Why not?" said Norman Adlam.

"Yeah, why not?" agreed Corky Corcoran. The other players shouted their agreement.

"Well, lad," said Terry Potts, "it looks like you've got yourself a job." He paused. "So long as your dad says it's OK, of course."

Swot looked anxiously at George Watson. His dad still looked as though he was in a trance. He said nothing, just nodded dumbly.

"Right!" announced Terry Potts. "That's decided! Jimmy Charlton has been replaced by Simon Watson! Rumney have got another manager!"

The dressing room was almost empty now. Sgt. Terry Potts had headed off to Rumney Police Station, taking PC Roland Cape with him. The other players had gone their separate ways.

Jack Pettigrew, not sure whether to laugh at

how he'd been taken in, or press charges because of it, had headed off to his palatial home for a palatial celebratory whisky.

Brian and Kev Murrant had left too. Brian's departure had been swift, once terms had been negotiated.

"No more threats, then?" he'd said to Kev and Swot.

"No," Swot had said.

"Not from me, bruv," said Kev. "My lips are sealed."

"No sabotaging this Sunday's car boot sale?"

"Nope."

"No stopping me from buying my replacement television and squaring things with the Wrinklies?"

"Definitely not," said Swot.

"Hallelujah," said Brian. "Come on, you," he'd said to Kev. "Let's go."

Kev had started to gather the UNCLE equipment together until Brian had stopped him. "Leave that, eh?"

"Why? It's a brilliant system."

"It's an illegal system," said Brian. "And I never want to see it again."

And so they'd gone, leaving Swot to gather together the UNCLE system and pack it into its holdall. Once they were alone George Watson finally broke his silence. "You substituted me," he said. He put his hands on his hips. "*You* substituted *me*!"

Swot looked as though he was appealing to a tough referee for mercy. "It was an accident, Dad! It looked like your ankle had gone. How did I know you'd only lost your boot?"

"Mmmm," said George Watson, unconvinced. "Well, let's forget about that for now. There's the other matter to deal with first."

"Other matter?"

"You took my job. I wanted to be Rumney manager."

"Dad, if I'd known you were going to ask Jack Pettigrew to be manager, I'd never have done it. Honest."

George Watson was looking stern. "But you didn't. And you did."

"Eh?"

"You didn't know I was going to ask Jack Pettigrew to be manager. And you did get it."

Swot nodded guiltily. "I know."

Looking down at the floor, Swot didn't see the smile as it spread slowly across his father's face. "And," beamed George Watson, "you did it really well!"

Swot was smiling himself now. "I did, didn't I?"

"You surely did! Son, I'm proud of you!" He gathered up his things and put his arm round Swot's shoulders. "Come on, let's go. We've got some talking to do."

"What about?"

"Tactics for the Lipton match, of course! Our last game of the season! I want my instructions, Son!"

Swot grinned at his father. "All right, then," he said happily. "First instruction. Don't call me 'Son'. Call me 'Boss'!"

# CHAPTER 15

## Swot Gets Choosy

"Picked the team for the Lipton match yet?" asked George Watson casually at the breakfast table next morning. "Boss," he added, with a smile.

"Not yet," said Swot. "It's only Wednesday, Dad. There might be some injuries from last night's game."

"Well," said George Watson pointedly, "you'll be pleased to know my dodgy ankle is definitely OK."

"It is?"

"A1 condition. Never felt better."

"Good," said Swot. But, somehow, he wasn't sure he meant it.

190

"What's the team, then?" asked Kev for the trillionth time. They were walking home from school, after a day during which it seemed to Swot that Kev had asked the same question every time he opened his mouth.

"I haven't decided," said Swot. "It's only Wednesday."

"What about tactics, then? You must've thought about tactics."

"Not really," lied Swot.

"Liar," said Kev. "What did you say to old man Pettigrew, eh? 'Lipton will need to win as well', you said. 'They'll be attacking us so we hit 'em on the break'."

"Something like that," shrugged Swot.

"So you have thought about tactics, then."

"OK. A bit."

"So you must've thought about the team."

"Why?"

"'Cos," said Kev, "even I know you need forwards who can run like the clappers to play that way."

"Probably," said Swot.

"Someone like Adie Mason."

"Possibly."

"Did well last night, didn't he? When he came on."

"Not bad."

"He was brilliant!"

"Like I said. Not bad."

"So is he in the team for Saturday?"

"It's only Wednesday. It's too early to say..."

Kev stopped and looked Swot in the eye. "Look, when you gonna face facts? You've got no choice. Terry Venables would do it."

"Do what?"

"Drop him, you've gotta drop him."

"Who?" said Swot.

"Who, who!" scoffed Kev. "You know who! Your old man! You've gotta leave him out."

"Rumney versus Lipton," said George Watson. "My 500th game. Amazing." He said it softly to himself, but loud enough for Swot to hear on the other side of the kitchen.

"Mmmm," said Swot, through a mouthful of toast. "Great."

"Sorted out the team yet?" asked George Watson.

"Not yet. It's only Thursday."

"Nobody's rung up to say they're injured. You've got a full squad to pick from by the looks of it."

"Looks like it."

"Pretty straightforward then."

"Pretty..." said Swot. "Only..."

"I know, Son," said George Watson. "Adie Mason. He's a bit of a problem. Right?"

"Er ... yes ... that's right."

"He did well when he came on Tuesday night. You must be tempted to leave him in."

"Maybe," said Swot. Had he guessed?

"But if you do that, you've got to leave out you-know-who," said George Watson.

Swot's eyebrows lifted. "I know," he said.

"And Baz Lucas won't like that. Not for an important game like this one. No, he won't like being left out one little bit."

"Baz Lucas?"

"Of course. A forward for a forward. I mean, there's nobody else you could leave out, is there?"

George Watson settled down on the other side of the breakfast table. "My last game, on Saturday. Five hundred appearances. It's a real milestone, Son. I'm going to be a proud man when I run out on to that pitch."

"Well?" asked Kev on the way home that evening. "What's the team?"

"It's only Thursday. I've got another couple of days to go yet."

"Chicken! You're chicken!"

"I am not!" said Swot. "It needs thinking about."

"Thinking!" scoffed Kev. "It don't need thinking about. You gotta leave him out!"

"I can feel the old butterflies already," said George Watson.

"You can?" mumbled Swot. He started buttering another piece of toast to avoid looking his dad in the eye.

"Yep. Amazing. They don't usually start until I shut the shop Saturday lunchtime. But here we are, only Friday morning, and they've started already."

"Dad. . ." began Swot. "About the game. . ."

"Big game, Son. Biggest for ages."

"I haven't decided on the team yet."

"Selection problems, eh? Don't worry. They're a good bunch. Whoever you leave out will take the decision like a man."

"He will?"

"Sure." He clapped Swot on the shoulder. "Have a good day at school, Son."

"Thanks," said Swot, his mind eased. "A busy day for you, is it?"

"Fairly, fairly. Not too busy to stop me cleaning the old boots today, though. Got to have 'em sparkling for the 500th, haven't I now?"

*    *    *

"Is that it?" said Kev. "Is it? The team?"

Swot nodded. In his hand fluttered a page torn from his English exercise book. Poetry had been a lost cause that Friday afternoon.

"Come on then," said Kev with a grab. "Gizza look."

Swot held the sheet of paper close to his chest. Kev backed away. "OK, OK. Read it out, then."

Swot held the page out. "Corcoran in goal."

"Surprise, surprise. Come on."

"Keith Burwood right back. Reuben Rix left back."

"Of course."

"Billy Wright and Jason Doggett, central defenders."

"Yeees! And..."

"Midfield – Polo Pirelli, Terry Potts, Norman Adlam and Tommy Thomas..."

"Front men! Who's up front?"

"Baz Lucas..."

"And!"

"And..." Swot hesitated.

Kev couldn't stand the tension any longer. With a lunge he grabbed the team sheet. "Chicken!" He was staring at the blank spot where the one remaining name should have been.

"I haven't decided yet! I've got until tomorrow!"

"You've gotta leave him out," yelled Kev. He pulled a pencil from his pocket and scrawled "Adie Mason" in the blank space, with "sub: George Watson" underneath. "There," he said, handing the sheet back. "You know it makes sense."

Swot shoved the page into his blazer pocket. "I..."

"Well?"

"I think I'll sleep on it," he said.


In fact, Swot hardly slept at all. He tossed and turned all night. As he lay in bed the next morning, gazing at the team sheet and action-replaying Rumney's last two games in his head, Swot knew his mind was made up.

Rumney's best moments had been when George Watson had either been out on the wing or in the dressing room. When his dad had been on the pitch he'd either fallen over the ball, given it away or blasted it out of the ground.

Kev was right. Adie Mason had to play. George Watson had to be the substitute. The only problem was ... when to tell him?

Now, Swot decided. Slowly he crept downstairs and into the kitchen.

He found it empty. Of course, he realized. His dad would be out in the van, making his deliveries good and early. With a sigh of relief, he went back up to his room to get dressed.

Later. He would tell him later.

Together with Mrs Young, Swot had been serving customers for most of the morning before the van pulled up outside.

"Dad..." said Swot as George Watson pushed open the shop door.

"Yes, Son?"

"Half a pound of carrots and two pounds of Granny Smiths' if you please, young man," interrupted a customer.

"I..."

"At once, if you don't mind! Some of us haven't got time to stand around talking all day!"

"Tell you later," said Swot.

George Watson nodded cheerfully and went through into the small back room which doubled as a store-room and office. By the time Swot had finished serving, George Watson was into his other regular Saturday morning job of doing his accounts. With a pencil in his hand and a calculator at his elbow, his dad was a bit too busy to be interrupted, Swot decided.

Later. He would tell him later.

No, he wouldn't. He would get it over and done with.

He edged towards the back room. He edged

away again. He moved forward again. Then, just as he was about to stride in and break the bad news, George Watson broke the pencil he was using and marched off to find another one.

No problem. He'd do what he'd thought first. Tell him later.

Another rush of customers began almost immediately and didn't die away until it was nearly one o'clock and time to close. Swot helped Mrs Young to sweep up, then bring in the display racks from the front of the shop. By the time she waved a cheery farewell and trundled down the road it was half-past one.

Only then did Swot realize that his dad hadn't returned to his books. He slid the bolts across the top and bottom of the shop door, flicked the "Closed" sign into place, and then walked through into the house.

No sign of George Watson.

Swot went upstairs and into his room.

Funny, he thought immediately. Something's different.

He looked around. Bedside table, bed, bookcase full of books – all there. Wardrobe door open, as he'd left it. The UNCLE holdall in the bottom of the wardrobe where he'd dumped it on Tuesday night – again, just as he'd left it. The Rumney team sheet on his bed, just as he'd left it. Next to it, his pencil sharpener. Just as he *hadn't* left it! That pencil sharpener had been in his school bag! "Oh no," he groaned to himself.

Had his dad come looking for a pencil sharpener? If he had ... had he seen the team sheet? The team sheet with Kev's hastily scrawled "sub: George Watson" on the bottom of it?

His question was answered sooner than he thought.

Behind him he heard his bedroom door click shut, followed by the scrape of a key turning in the lock.

Swot leapt across to the door and rattled the handle. "Dad! Is that you?"

Silence. He rattled at the door handle again. "Let me out!"

"Sorry, Son," said George Watson's voice from the other side of the door. "It looks like one of us has got to miss this game. And it isn't going to be me."

"Dad!!"

"See you later," said George Watson. "Boss."

Swot sank down on to his bed.

He'd been substituted. By the substitute.

# CHAPTER 16

## The Great Escape

For the first time in his young life, Swot found himself wishing he hadn't always asked for a football book for his birthday and Christmas presents.

Why couldn't he have been interested in how door locks worked, or in the science of escapology? Then he might have had something to help him in his present predicament. Films, he thought frantically. How did people escape in films? Climb out of the window and slide down a rope made out of sheets!

No good, he thought, looking at his duvet. And the drop was too big to try jumping.

He spotted the drainpipe which ran down from the gutter above his bedroom window. Could he chance it? He tried to open the window. Stuck. No, locked! His dad had thought of everything. He couldn't even scream for help.

He launched himself at the bedroom door. Worse than useless. The door didn't move, and he ended up with a shoulder that felt as though it had been hit by a truck.

Across the road an alarm began to wail. Swot sat on the floor with his head in his hands. He felt like wailing himself.

George Watson and Sergeant Terry Potts arrived at the Rumney ground within seconds of each other. "In a hurry, isn't he?" said George Watson as, seconds after dropping off Terry Potts, PC Roland Cape screeched out of the car park and off down the road.

"Alarm call," said Potts. "Roland loves 'em. Gives him a chance to do his Nigel Mansell act." He peered into George

Watson's van. "Where's our young manager then, George?"

"Er ... he's ... er ... gonna be a bit late."

"Nothing wrong?"

"Well..." said George Watson, "he was definitely feeling a bit sick when I left him."

And feeling sicker by the minute. Swot's final idea had failed. Ten minutes spent trying to pick the lock on his door with a bent wire coathanger had been a complete failure. The door was still locked as ever.

He opened his wardrobe door, threw the coathanger on top of the UNCLE holdall in disgust, and sank dejectedly on to his bed.

"Oh, shut up!" he muttered. Outside, the alarm was still ringing. It would be the village hall alarm. It always was. Nobody took much notice of it. It had been going off at least once a week since it was installed and never once because a burglar had got in. Nine times out of ten it was warning the world that the cleaner had gone home and forgotten to take her cat with her.

Swot looked out of his window as the alarm jangled on. Any minute now the police would turn up and sort things out...

The police!! In a panda car! With a radio! A radio that picked up UNCLE transmissions!

Swot dived into his wardrobe and frantically started to unpack the UNCLE holdall.

It had been a fun afternoon for PC Roland Cape.

A quick dash from the Rumney football ground to the Rumney village hall, his siren wailing importantly. Then he'd had to find the hall key. It hadn't been in its usual flowerpot and he'd had to use a bit of detective work before locating it under the doormat.

Finally he'd turned the alarm off.

Now it was time to report the series of successes. He flicked on the car's two-way radio. "ZB to control room, ZB to control room."

"Come in ZB. What was it, Roly?"

"The usual. Cat problem. What now?"

"Emergency! Emergency!"

"What!" said Roland Cape. "Great! Where?"

"Where, what?"

"The emergency! Where is it?"

"Who said anything about an emergency?" said Control.

"You did."

"I didn't."

"Emergency!" yelled the radio again.

Roland Cape was getting annoyed. "Come on, Control, stop playing the fool!"

"Playing the fool!" answered Control. "What do you mean, playing the fool? Wait till I get my hands on you, Cape, and you'll find out who's playing the fool..."

"Can you hear me? I'm locked in! Watson the greengrocer's! Come and get me out! It's an emergency!"

PC Roland Cape's memory didn't let him down. It had been trained for situations like this. "UNCLE," he muttered, as he started the panda car.

Wristwatch, stop watch, pencil, notebook, red card, yellow card. "All present and correct," said the man in black to himself.

A head popped around the changing-room door. It was followed by an arm, a hand and a sheet of paper. They all belonged to the Lipton United manager. "Afternoon, Ref. Lipton team sheet."

"Thanks."

"Not too late?"

"No, you're in good time." The referee looked at his wristwatch. "Mind you, the Rumney manager had better get a move on."

Getting a move on was what PC Roland Cape really enjoyed about being a PC. And he seemed to be getting more chances to do it on this one afternoon than he usually got in a week. "Woo-woo!" he went, in time with the panda car siren.

Outside, cars pulled over to let him go by. Old ladies covered their ears. Children pointed and bicyclists wobbled.

While in the back seat, checking his watch as the seconds ticked by, Swot held his breath.

"Looks like our young manager's going to be late," said Terry Potts. "Somebody'd better take the team sheet along to the Ref."

George Watson stood up. "I'll do it," he said. "Same starting line-up as usual, eh?" He turned as he reached the dressing-room door.

"I mean, he wouldn't want to change a winning team, would he?"

George walked along the short corridor which led to the cramped changing room the referee used. He knocked on the door.

"Rumney team sheet, Ref!" he called.

The door half opened. The man in black looked confused.

"What?"

"Rumney team sheet," repeated George Watson.

"Playing two teams, are you?" asked the referee.

"Eh?" It was George Watson's turn to be confused.

The referee waved a sheet of paper that George Watson recognized: a sheet which had "sub: George Watson" written at the bottom of it.

"Who gave you that?"

"Your manager," said the referee. "Ask him yourself." He opened the door fully.

"Sorry, Dad," said Swot.

# CHAPTER 17

## Super-Sub!

The match kicked off in silence. Silence, that was, from the Rumney bench.

Swot said nothing. On his left, Kev didn't like to say anything until Swot said something. And on Swot's right, waiting for somebody to say something so he could bite his head off, sat a furious George Watson.

The silence was finally broken after ten minutes' play, as Keith Burwood made a good interception and laid the ball inside to Terry Potts. Without looking up, the burly police sergeant walloped the ball forward high to Baz Lucas. Lucas played a glancing header on to Adie Mason.

"There goes the March Hare," muttered George Watson sourly as Adie Mason sprinted down the wing. "Watch him run into trouble."

But Mason didn't run into trouble. He ran into the Lipton half of the field, completely outpacing his marker, and on to the edge of the penalty area. "Return ball!" screamed Swot, as Baz Lucas sprinted into space on the right.

"He won't see him," said George Watson.

But he was wrong. Adie Mason looked up and slipped a delightful ball to Baz Lucas.

"Good ball," shouted Kev.

"Luck," said George Watson.

"Hit it!" yelled Swot.

"Goal... No! Oh!" yelled Kev as Baz Lucas' shot smacked against the post and bounced away to safety.

"Rubbish," said George Watson. "I'd have had that."

"Yeah," muttered Kev. "Over the bar."

Out on the pitch another Lipton move had broken down. Norman Adlam fed the ball out to Adie Mason again. Mason was playing out of his skin. He sidestepped one lunging tackle, then another.

"Watch," said George Watson, "he'll lose it."

But Adie Mason didn't lose it. He went on. With the Lipton defence retreating desperately, he cut inside. Baz Lucas made a dummy run, taking a defender with him. Dashing into the open space, Mason suddenly found himself with only the goalkeeper to beat.

"Hit it, Adie!" yelled Kev.

"He must score," cried Swot.

"He won't," said George Watson.

He didn't either – because he was fouled. As Adie Mason pulled back his right foot to shoot, he found his left foot going up in the air as well, as a desperate Lipton defender dived in to tackle him.

"Penalty, Ref!"

"Yeah!" chanted Kev as the referee pointed to the spot. "Rumney! Rumney!"

"Come on, Pottsie," muttered Swot as

Sergeant Terry Potts placed the ball on the penalty spot with the sort of care he normally reserved only for the Chief Superintendent's cap. "Bang it in."

Terry Potts strode up to the ball. Wilcox, the Lipton goalie, decided to go to his left and hope for the best.

To his left he went, just as Terry Potts kicked the ball. Immediately he realized he'd guessed wrong. The ball was heading dead straight, into the centre of the goal. Despairingly, Wilcox stuck out a toe as he continued his dive.

"Oh, no!" said Kev. "He's missed it."

The ball had struck Wilcox on the toe and ballooned up and over the bar.

"I don't believe it," said Swot. He buried his head in his hands. For a moment complete silence descended on the Rumney bench again.

It was broken by a loud bellow. "Bad luck, Pottsie! Come on, lads!"

Swot looked up. He smiled as the man with the number 12 on his shirt shook his fist at the

Rumney players and yelled. "Come on, lads! You can do it!!"

George Watson was back!

Not all the Rumney players shared George Watson's confidence, though. At half-time the mood in the dressing room was downright miserable.

"We should be at least two up," grumbled Norman Adlam.

"Dunno how he saved that penalty," muttered Terry Potts.

"Luck," said George Watson, "pure luck. Right, Son?"

Swot nodded. "I reckon so."

Norman Adlam glowered. "So what about all the other chances we've had then?" He waved a finger at Baz Lucas and Adie Mason. "Our strikers on strike, are they?"

"Come off it, Norman!" said Lucas. "The ball just hasn't been running for us today."

"We're trying," said Adie Mason.

"You can say that again," moaned Adlam. "Very trying."

Baz Lucas jumped to his feet. "Just watch it, you!"

George Watson leapt between them. "Normie, Baz, come on! Arguing won't do any good, will it?"

"We're all over them," said Swot. "Lipton haven't carved out a single chance."

"The manager's right," said George Watson. "He's been right all along." He looked at Swot as he went on. "He was right to make me sub, because I've been playing rubbish. I should have accepted his decision, and not been such an idiot. And his tactics have been right," he said, turning quickly back to the Rumney players. "So keep playing the way you are and the goals will come."

Norman Adlam looked far from convinced. "They'd better. In case anyone's forgotten, we've got to win this game. Lipton only have to draw."

"Nobody's forgotten, Normie," said George Watson. "So come on, let's go out there and win it!"

Rumney swept forward straight from the kick-off. A raking pass from Norman Adlam found Keith Burwood overlapping down the right.

"Use it," snarled Adlam.

Burwood used it. Chipping the ball into the path of Baz Lucas he ran forward for the return ball. It came to him perfectly, just as a Lipton defender had committed himself to an interception he couldn't make. Burwood got the ball under control and shot in one movement.

It looked a goal all the way . . . until it struck the referee on the back of the head and ricocheted straight into the Lipton goalie's arms.

"You idiot!" yelled Norman Adlam as Burwood trudged back.

"Who're you calling an idiot?" retorted Burwood. "Was it my fault the ref got in the way?"

"You should have known he was going to be there!" yelled Norman Adlam, his hands on his hips.

Burwood stopped to argue. "How?" he shouted back, "I'm a defender, not a mind-reader!"

"Well, you could have fooled me!"

"Get back!"

The yell came from Terry Potts. While Adlam and Burwood were standing in the middle of the pitch arguing, the Lipton goalie had thrown the ball out. Lipton were attacking through the gap they'd left. In an instant the Rumney defence found themselves out-numbered.

Terry Potts, without Keith Burwood alongside him, suddenly found himself against two Lipton attackers. He went towards the one with the ball. The Lipton player waited, then slipped the ball to his now unmarked colleague. Desperately Corky Corcoran came off his line in an attempt to narrow the angle, but it was too late. The Lipton player simply sidefooted the ball past him and into the net.

"One down," said Kev dumbly. "We're one down."

"All the play," said Swot. "We've had all

the play, and we're one down."

"We've had it," said Kev.

"No, we haven't," snapped George Watson. He leapt from the dug-out and marched up and down the touchline. "Heads up, lads!" he yelled. "Come on! We can do it!"

From where Swot was sitting, the lads clearly didn't think they could. They almost went two down immediately, as a miserable-looking Norman Adlam gave up chasing the Lipton player he was supposed to be marking and allowed him to run through for a shot which missed Corky Corcoran's post by inches.

"Their heads have gone down," muttered Kev.

Swot held his own head in his hands. Kev was right. The goal seemed to have knocked the stuffing out of them.

He racked his brains. Rumney had never played like this before. Even during their worst games they'd never given up trying.

Why now? Why today?

What was the difference?

"Come on, lads! Let's go! Come on! Keep playing!" George Watson's yell caused Swot to look up. Of course! *That* was the difference!

George Watson – enthusiastic, bustling, never-say-die George Watson – wasn't playing!

"Dad!" he called. "Get ready! You're going on!"

"What?" said Kev. "How's that gonna help?"

"By giving Rumney what they're missing, that's how!"

George Watson was ready in a flash. "Who are you bringing off, Son? Adie Mason or Baz Lucas? They're both playing well. Better'n I've done all season."

"Can't argue with that," said Kev.

"Neither of them," said Swot. "You're going on for Norman Adlam."

"Normie?" George Watson's mouth fell open. "You want me to play midfield? Me?"

"Him? Midfield?" echoed Kev.

George Watson looked just as amazed. "What can I do in midfield?"

"Just be yourself, Dad."

"Oh, gawd," muttered Kev.

George Watson looked at Swot. "What d'you mean?"

"Enthusiasm, Dad! That's what Rumney need now. Just get on there, and fire 'em up, Dad!"

Kev was shaking his head in amazement. "It's working. I think it's working."

Next to him in the dug-out, Swot's heart was thumping. "Come on, Dad," he muttered.

Slowly, Rumney were stirring themselves. And it was all due to George Watson. Since coming on, he had run around like a maniac. He'd hardly touched the ball, but that wasn't the point. Simply by dashing about he'd made things happen. More than once a Lipton player had given the ball away simply because he'd found George Watson breathing down his neck.

Even a sudden cloudburst hadn't dampened his spirits. He'd just ploughed on, wiping the raindrops from the end of his nose before yelling encouragement to somebody. "Go for it, Baz! Come on, Adie, move yourself! Pottsie, tackle him!"

Now, the Watson spirit was spreading throughout the Rumney team. As if to prove it, Polo Pirelli won the ball with a crushing tackle in the middle of the field. "Good tackle," said Kev.

Swot checked his watch. "Ten minutes to go."

"Something's got to happen soon," said Kev. "Oh! Bad ball, Polo! Who's gonna catch that?"

Pirelli, after his great tackle, had badly overhit his through pass to Baz Lucas. As the ball skidded over the wet grass towards the corner flag, Lucas didn't even bother to give chase.

A Lipton defender came across, intending to shadow the ball into touch. Then he, too, decided it was a lost cause and slowed to a walk. It would waste a bit more time.

Only one person kept going. George Watson galloped past Baz Lucas as the striker stopped running. Moments later the Lipton defender was overtaken by what he thought for a moment was a runaway train. "No chance," he said to George Watson's back as the Rumney man charged by.

"He won't catch that," said Kev. "A racehorse couldn't catch that."

Swot agreed. "Save your energy, Dad," he yelled.

They were all wrong. As the ball neared the corner flag it started to slow. Then, amazingly, it stopped dead.

"He *is* going to get it!" yelled Swot. "Baz!! Baz!! Into the area! Fast!"

As George Watson got the ball under control, Baz Lucas hared into the Lipton penalty area. With the dawdling Lipton defender out of position, Wilcox, the Lipton goalkeeper, was forced to cover the near post. When George Watson's cross came over, all Lucas had to do was let it bounce off his head and into the net.

"Goal!!" yelled Kev. "Yahoo!!"

"Two minutes," hollered Swot. "Two minutes left! Keep it going, Dad!!"

Lipton kicked off. George dived into the tackle again, and again, and again, as the Lipton players passed the ball back to their goalkeeper, Wilcox.

"Time-wasting, Ref!" yelled Swot.

"They only need the draw," said Kev. "Of course they're gonna waste time."

As the ball came to him, Wilcox took careful aim and walloped it straight into touch. "More time-wasting," groaned Kev. "We're not gonna do it."

Swot leapt up from the bench. "Go up, Terry!" he yelled to Terry Potts. "We've got to go for the winner!"

Keith Burwood took the throw. He lobbed it gently to Polo Pirelli. Pirelli saw that George Watson was in space on the halfway line and shaped to pass to him. "Not me, I'm finished," gasped George Watson. He sank slowly to his knees.

"Polo!" screamed Terry Potts, surging

forward. "Let's have it!" When Terry Potts said "Let's have it" like that, he wasn't joking. Polo Pirelli let him have it. The burly Rumney captain set off with the ball at his feet and a determined look on his face.

He surged past one Lipton defender, then another. A third defender put in a half-hearted challenge and ended up face down in the mud.

With the other Lipton defenders hesitating as he reached the edge of the Lipton penalty area, Terry Potts looked up. He had a clear shooting chance. It was now or never.

"Oooomph!" grunted the Rumney captain as he hit quite the hardest shot of his career.

How Wilcox in the Lipton goal managed to get a finger to it, nobody knew. But with an almighty leap he did, and it was enough to divert a shot that was whistling into the top corner slightly upwards.

Thwaack!

Terry Potts' heart fell as the ball smacked against the crossbar and, such was the power of his shot, sailed back over his head towards midfield.

226

"That's it," said Kev. "Look. The ref's checking his watch."

But Swot wasn't looking at the referee. He was looking at the exhausted figure kneeling in midfield, and the ball that was bouncing towards him. "Get up, Dad!" he yelled.

George Watson dragged himself to his feet and, with one final effort, moved towards the bouncing ball. As his dad ran, memories of the season seemed to pass before Swot's eyes like a giant action-replay. Memories of his dad, running in just as he was now, and blasting a shot miles over the crossbar.

But ... that had always been from the edge of the area. Now he was in midfield.

In midfield! Swot leapt to his feet.

"Shoot, Dad!!" he screamed.

Without thinking, George Watson gathered his remaining strength together and hammered the ball towards the Lipton goal.

The ball rose rapidly. As it passed the point where the goal usually was when George Watson had a shot, it was still way up in the air. But today wasn't usual. Today, the goal was much further off. And the ball was starting to come down.

Down and down it came.

Down and down, as Swot held his breath.

Down and down, as twenty-one players gazed at it, unable to reach it even if they'd used a trampoline.

Down and down, as the twenty-second player, Wilcox in the Lipton goal, stopped nursing the finger that had tipped Terry Potts' thunderbolt on to the crossbar, and charged back across his goal.

Down and down as Wilcox flung himself at it desperately.

Down and down.

And down.

Into the net.

# CHAPTER 18

## Final Whistle

From the scale of the celebrations in the dressing room, anyone would have thought that Rumney had just won the F.A. Cup, instead of merely staving off relegation from the First Division of the South Hampshire League.

Jack Pettigrew arrived with bottles of champagne and a pile of plastic beakers. Sgt. Terry Potts got to his feet and severely warned all present about the perils of drinking and driving. Then he cracked open the first bottle, scoring a direct hit on the back of Norman Adlam's head with the cork.

"First thing he's headed all season!" shouted somebody.

As the champagne was handed round, George Watson grabbed a beaker for himself and a small one for Swot. Together they went and sat in a corner.

"Well done, Son," said George Watson, lifting his beaker. "Here's to you."

Swot lifted his own beaker. "And you, Dad." He smiled. "Super–Sub!"

George Watson grinned. "Ah, but you put me on. And yelled at the right time. I'd never have had that shot if you hadn't shouted."

"I didn't tell you to chase that ball for the first goal, though," said Swot. "I never expected you to catch it."

"Nobody did," said Kev, who'd grabbed a champagne bottle for himself. "It was amazing the way it stopped dead like that."

"No it wasn't," said George Watson. "I knew it would. That's why I went after it."

"You knew it would?" said Swot.

"Course," said George Watson. "We'd just had a downpour, hadn't we?"

"Yes. But I'd have expected that to make the ball run faster."

George Watson shook his head. "Not down in that corner, Son. After five hundred games for Rumney I know that pitch out there like the back of my hand. There's a little hollow in that corner, and water runs into it pretty quick. When I saw the ball going that way, I just reckoned it might get stuck in there – and it did."

"The man's a genius," said Kev. "Haven't I always said so?"

"Not always," smiled Swot.

"Not a bad way to go out," said George Watson. He got to his feet and called for silence.

"Quiet!" yelled Norman Adlam. "George wants to tell us about his goal."

Everybody laughed. Corky Corcoran shouted, "You're not going to tell us we've got to wait another five hundred games for the next one, are you?"

George Watson shook his head. "No, Corky, I'm not."

"It's going to take him six hundred games instead!" laughed Terry Potts.

"No, it's not," said George Watson. "Because I won't be playing any more games for Rumney at all." He looked around at his team-mates. "I've decided to hang up my boots. This was a great way to finish. But from now on I'm just going to be a spectator."

"No, tha's not."

All heads turned towards the doorway. Jack Pettigrew, wealthy butcher and Chairman of Rumney Town, stepped forward. "Tha's not going to be a spectator, George."

George Watson frowned. "Why not?"

"Tha'll be sitting on t'Rumney bench, that's why."

"As sub? I've just said I'm not going to play again."

Swot got there first. He looked at Jack Pettigrew. "You mean..."

"Ah!" said the Rumney Chairman. "At least somebody round here's with it." He turned to George Watson. "Not as sub, George! As manager!"

George Watson was speechless. His mouth opened, but no words came out.

"You still want the job, I take it?"

"Yes! Yes! He does!" It was Swot, happier than he'd ever been in his life. "He accepts."

Jack Pettigrew nodded slowly. "Good." He held out his hand to Swot. "Ah want to thank you for your efforts for Rumney, young man..."

"Even if they did make me look daft," called out somebody.

"Even if they did make me look daft," echoed Jack Pettigrew, with a smile. "But the get-up-and-go your dad showed out there this afternoon convinced me that he's the man for t'job."

Swot nodded. "I agree!"

Even Kev nodded.

"Although," said Jack Pettigrew, "I'd like to hear him accept it for himself."

"The answer's no, Mr Pettigrew..." said George Watson, finally finding his voice.

"Eh?" exclaimed Jack Pettigrew.

"Dad!" cried Swot.

"...Unless you agree to one condition," said George Watson. "If you do, fine. I'll take it. If not ... you'll have to look for somebody else."

"Dad!" cried Swot. "You can't mean it!"

"I do mean it," said George Watson.

Jack Pettigrew frowned. "Condition?" he said slowly. "What ... condition?" he said.

Swot looked up at his dad. George Watson looked pretty serious. But not for long. Slowly a smile spread across his face.

"I want an assistant," he said, putting his arm around Swot's shoulders. "Someone to help me with tactics."

Jack Pettigrew looked thoughtful, but when he turned towards Swot his eyes were twinkling.

"Reet! Agreed!"